*Another one for my wife POH-TUAN*
*The loveliest lady I have ever known*
*She is my life*

*Koh-Eet-Senko*

# Koh-Eet-Senko

## GRANT GALL

SHIELD PRESS

First published in Great Britain 2003 by
Shield Press
Colchester, Essex

Copyright © 2002 by Grant Gall

ISBN 0-9505068-1-8

Set in Palatino by
Rowland Phototypesetting Ltd
Printed in Great Britain by
St Edmundsbury Press Ltd
both of Bury St Edmunds, Suffolk

# Acknowledgements

To Jack and Sue Place of Fort Morgan, Colorado, for their ever willing, generous hospitality and much valued friendship. To Ken Hebenstreit, Nigel Craig, Alistair Wilde and Stephen Mina for their support and encouragement.

Also to Dr Nick Dixon, Dr Mark Aitken, Dr Charles Bodmer, Mr John Corr, Sister Ros Stacey, Sister Susie Nichol, Nettie Nichol and their dedicated teams without whom . . .

# *Contents*

# Author's Note

*Koh-Eet-Senko* is a novel based on the tragic final years of the Kiowa nation. It never wittingly strays from the path of recorded history. Leading figures on all sides lived and, in some instances, died as described. Their major utterances are often direct quotes translated and preserved as they were spoken. It is the author's sincere hope that he has written justly of them for good or bad or degrees between. The other characters who appear in the story within a story, are creations of his imagination.

# KOH-EET-SENKO

# *Prologue*

SHAD WALKER
1840?–1923
ALL-ROUND COWMAN
AND LOYAL FRIEND

We shuffled our freezing feet in embarrassed silence as we stood knee-deep in the mountain snows, staring down at the gnarled wooden board that marked the grave of Shad Walker. Everyone from our ranch was there. Not just as a matter of duty or even simple courtesy. But because we had all respected, and, in our own way, even loved the grizzled old cowhand whom we had just buried following his death from pneumonia. Pneumonia he had contracted while out looking for stray calves during an unexpected blizzard. That was Shad's way.

The others were embarrassed because, although Shad had been with us for almost thirty years, they knew so very little about him. I was embarrassed because I knew almost everything about him but dare not say any of the words that kept invading my thoughts. At last I turned to my father and said, 'Pa, it's your ranch and you were the first one among us who ever set eyes on him so you ought to say something over his grave. It doesn't seem right somehow to bury a man and then not say anything about him. Particularly a man like Shad.'

Dad wiped the tears from his eyes with the back of his glove. 'Damn wind plays havoc with your vision at this height,' he remarked hoarsely. He coughed as if to clear his throat of some obstruction. 'Son, it's almighty hard to say words over a man who's been your close friend for so many years but about whom you know so goddam little.' He looked upwards. 'Please excuse my blaspheming Lord but I'm sure you understand.'

He lowered his face again and looked at the grave. 'Perhaps it's enough for us just to have known him. He left his mark on us all. Me most of all because he helped me build this ranch right from nothing. He was always there. Always helping. Always ready to keep right on going when any normal man would have given in. But Shad wasn't any normal man. He never bothered you with his personal problems – if he had any.

'He was Mexican. That's obvious to all of us with eyes and ears. But he had an American name. He never told me how this came to be. And I never asked him. He never even told me what Shad stood for although I guessed it was Shadrack.

'What I recall most readily about him was the night I first ran into him. It was a bad winter that first year. I had registered my land claim and had started to make good on it by buying a few cattle, putting 'em out to graze and building a small cabin. More like a line shack than a cabin I guess. But it provided some protection against the cold. That night, however, it was freezing hard enough to drive a brass monkey clear out of his mind with anxiety. So I built the fire up. Too damn high in fact because the cabin burned down. I just stood there cursing like mad for being so bloody careless and helpless.

'Then out of the night rides this Mexican. He climbs off his horse and walks over. Before I realise what he is doing, the son-of-a-gun is calmly warming his hands against the flames. "Such camp fire hospitality is seldom to be found on such a lavish scale in these parts sēnor," he says quietly. I walks across, boiling over with temper and more than ready to bust him one. He just flashes me a grin which shows up so white in the light of the fire and says: "Not tonight sēnor. We are both tired and we will both need our strength to rebuild your cabin tomorrow." Somehow I believed him.

'Anyway we both shacks down in blankets from his bedroll and falls asleep by the blazing cabin. Next morning he is still there. He helped me put up a new, and better, cabin. And he's been right here with me ever since. Of his life I only know what happened from then on but never what took place before. And that when he died he wanted to be buried way up in these mountains so that he could look out across the land he loved.

'All in all perhaps that's what it boils down to. That just to have known one Shad Walker and to have had him as a friend, is more than enough in any one man's life.' Pa cleared his throat again. 'That's all I have to say; except "Thank you Shad" from all of us.'

And for all of us it was a long, hard, silent and, somehow, lonely ride back to the ranch, which we reached late that evening. With Shad's death a part of the ranch itself had died. Although in his eighties, we had all regarded him as indestructible. Now he was gone.

I promised myself, however, that I would return one day soon for a last goodbye to the best friend I ever had, then or later. He had wished to be buried deep in the recesses of the wilderness so that the face of the land around would remain as he had known it when he had ridden across its many features – all unscarred by civilisation. He had once told me that he wished to be buried where no man would ever find or disturb the peace of his last resting place. I would ask his forgiveness for my intrusion when I returned for my final farewell which had to be made alone. There were no feelings of guilt within me for I knew Shad would understand. He always had.

Shad had been like an uncle to me. He had even helped to deliver me when I was born, pa once told me after having one drink too many to control his tongue. 'But for God's sake don't tell your ma boy!' he had ordered. 'Or Shad either! Or anybody at all! Neither of them would ever forgive me for telling you. They hate like hell for Shad's role as midwife to be revealed to the world in general and to you in particular.' And he had let loose a mighty guffaw for some reason which he chose never to tell me.

For me Shad Walker had been every boy's dream of an uncle. He'd been a born storyteller. He had been so many places. Met so many people. And done so many things.

But the best story of them all he'd related to me during the vacation following my graduation from high school several years back when I'd told him that I had selected the study of the American Indian as a basis for my proposed academic qualifications in history. And that I intended to fight for the rights of all Indians once I had worked my way through college towards that same end.

And old Shad had known better than anyone that I would make that fight. He had watched me grow up tough and determined. In fact he'd had a big hand in making the mould from which I had been cast. He'd also known that some of my best friends had been young Indian students, who were having one hell of a struggle for the right to learn white men's professions in white men's schools in a country governed by white men for the benefit of white men. They'd been the main reason behind my decision not to follow my father into ranching – much to his chagrin. But I knew dad was proud of me for wanting to make my own stand in life just as he had made his all those years back in the wilderness which had been, and in many ways still was, Texas.

Before revealing his story to me, however, Shad told me that it was for the furtherance of my studies alone that he was relating it. And that I must first vow never to tell anyone of his involvement in what he was about to reveal. I so promised. And as a man of my word I never have betrayed, and never will betray, his trust in me.

But the story can be told without involving Shad in any way and I am sure he would never have objected to me retelling it with this in mind. In fact, I am certain that he would have approved; for it marks the beginning of my fight for the rights of the American Indians now that my years at college are behind me.

The book which you are about to read is Shad's account, as close to his words as my memory permits, of the destruction of a people. A primitive race which was crushed out of its nomadic existence – not by other uncivilised savages set upon an orgy of genocide. But by people very much like you and me. Some of them were, in fact, related to some of us. Of that there can be no doubt. There were parents, grandparents, and even great grandparents among them. And so some of us are their direct descendants. In their place we would probably have behaved very much as they did.

Whatever, they all had one common bond – a greed for land. And it was the encroachment of those landgrabbing white invaders upon the red man's territory in the latter half of the nineteenth century that led to Shad telling me, in such vivid and minute detail, of all that occurred during those years.

The territory for which the whites fought is that which we now call Texas. The people whose way of life was destroyed for all time were the Kiowas.

# Chapter One

The gigantic groping blood-red fingers of the dying sun reached feebly out across the land as if trying to clasp hold of the rocks to prevent itself from sinking beneath the world's edge which was the distant horizon. The ageing Kiowa chief, Satank, whose name means Sitting Bear, watched the death throes of the drowning sun. But he knew that it would be reborn from the world of darkness the following dawn with its vigour intact. Whereas he, Satank, whose seventieth summer was drawing near, would be one sun closer to death.

How was it, he pondered, that time had never been of import to the Indians of America until the arrival of the white man. White people had to have all things in neatly arranged compartments; each one labelled clearly. Not only time; but land, wealth and, saddest of all, people. And that was why each day left to him was so vital if he was to prevent the American government from putting his people, the Kiowas, into yet another of these boxes. Boxes which became smaller and more suffocating each time they and their brothers, the Comanches, signed a new treaty with the whites.

In seven suns, called one week by the white people, the five tribes of the Southern Plains – the Kiowas, Comanches, Southern Cheyennes, Arapahoes and Kiowa-Apaches – were to meet at a place called Medicine Lodge to discuss just one more such treaty with the Americans. But there will be no discussions, he thought. Just words that lasted shorter than the life of the smallest insect. For all the treaties they had signed thus far with the white man's government had always resulted in the Americans achieving their desires. But never the Kiowas.

This time, however, he hoped it would be different. That was why he had called a meeting of his tribe to take place, in the heart of their homeland, the northern grasslands of Texas, that night. On the Llano Estacado, or 'Staked Plain' in the American tongue, it was always much easier to talk when the sun had left the sky. For men's words frequently appeared as if heated by the sun itself. Whereas the night often seemed to bring with it a coolness of reasoning. Satank hoped that such would be the case tonight.

The old man watched with pride as the six military societies of the Kiowa tribe slowly assembled from all points of the compass. There were the Rabbits, the youngest and least tried of the warriors. Then came the Young Mountain Sheep, Crazy Horses, Black Legs and Horse Caps. These were all much the same in prestige and were all experienced fighters.

The ten most trusted and seasoned warriors of the entire tribe, however, formed an elite fighting brotherhood. They were the Chief Dogs or Koh-eet-senko. For any warrior to become a Koh-eet-senko was the greatest honour that could be bestowed upon him. Most men never knew such status for there could be only ten Chief Dogs at any one time. Satank was the oldest and most respected of the Koh-eet-senko.

The sun had now left the sky completely. Throughout the encampment twinkling fires were springing to life.

And there was an animated buzz of indistinguishable conversations as many people talked excitedly at the same time among their own small groups.

The flames leaping from the fire, in front of which Satank was seated, etched clearly upon his face the lines put there by his many years and the extreme climate which turned Texas into a fiery furnace in the summer and a set of freezing fangs in the winter.

The chief's features were strongly Mongolian in appearance. And he had a vanity rare among American Indians. He had a moustache. Virtually all Indians plucked out any facial hairs with tweezers. But not Satank. He stroked its long, greying strands thoughtfully while waiting for Satanta to arrive.

Satanta, or White Bear, was the only other chief to command a respect among the Kiowa people equal to that given to Satank. Although Satanta was about twenty years younger than Satank, the two men were like brothers. They were the unchallenged leaders of the Koh-eet-senko. Between them they led the entire Kiowa nation.

A burly, moon-faced man, Satanta had a zest for life that was truly remarkable even among the free-ranging Kiowas. However, the white invaders of his homeland were soon to change that and history would record his name as the most feared among all the Southern Plains Indians.

Satank and Satanta now led the Kiowas because their great chief, Dohasan, called Little Mountain by the Americans, had died in the summer of that year, 1867. And his successor, Guipago, or Lone Wolf, although a formidable warrior, was unable to control the Kiowas as Dohasan had done. So the leadership had soon drifted into the

11

hands of those gifted with the force of character necessary to bind any people together as one.

Thus, by the fall of that same year, the reins guiding
the Kiowas were firmly in the dual grasp of Satank and
Satanta.

Satanta was among the last to arrive at the council. As
he sat upon the earth at the side of his friend Satank, the
latter turned to him and murmured, 'Middle-aged men
should not have pretty young wives. Such women make
them forgetful of other things.'

'Other things than what?' asked his comrade with
feigned innocence.

'That thing which makes a man forget all other things
and turns strong warriors into toys for women.'

'You say this because you are jealous and yearn for
that which the years have taken from you.'

Satank's expression changed to one of complacence.
'Only death can take that from me', he said contentedly.
'It is just that I enjoy my pleasures early in the morning.'

Satanta grunted. And grinned. Was this playful cross-
talk not always how it should be among friends.

Satank rose slowly to his feet. As soon as he stood up
so the hubbub around him died as abruptly as a snuffed
flame. Soon, the entire camp was silent. With most Indian
tribes age brought respect. And the Kiowas were no different from the majority where the privileges of age were
concerned. Everyone waited for Satank, the oldest Koh-
eet-senko, to speak.

Like all Plains Indians, the Kiowas were fond of oratory. And Satank was no exception. He savoured the
moment to its fullest before breaking the silence with his
carefully chosen words.

'In a short time we will go, together with our Comanche brothers and other tribes, to a place which the white men call Medicine Lodge. They want us to sign yet another treaty. But, if we agree to do so, it will not be long before they break it just as they have broken the many others we have signed in years past. To the Americans treaties are just an easy way of depriving us of more and more land. How many treaties will it take before we are forced into the desert and inevitable warfare against the Apaches whose homeland it is?

'Why should we kill one another when it is the Americans we should be fighting? Many of us were at the soldier chief's council five moons ago when Walks-Like-A-Shadow, who speaks a little of the white man's tongue, heard the big blue-coat general tell the other blue-coats around him that, although the Kiowas were the smallest of the southern tribes, we possessed an inborn deadliness which made us more dangerous, man for man, than any other Indians anywhere on the plains.'

As he spoke so several of the people around Walks-Like-A-Shadow turned to look at this man referred to by the great Satank. Walks-Like-A-Shadow, a handsome young warrior in his mid-twenties, straightened his shoulders at this unexpected attention. Although a tall, strongly built man, he could stalk animals, birds and people alike with an uncanny silence to his movements. That was how he had earned his name. That was how he had got close enough to the American general to hear his words. A member of the Crazy Horses military society, Walks-Like-A-Shadow had but one burning major ambition in his life. To become a member of the Koh-eet-senko.

'This general also said that when the size of our nation of less than two thousand people was taken into

13

consideration we had probably killed more Americans, man for man, than any other tribe in the entire West,' continued Satank. 'That is why they want us to continue agreeing to their treaties – so that no more white people will die at the hands of the Kiowa.

'Yet these Americans will not settle the issue for all time by fighting us man to man. Each time we are called to a treaty meeting we are surrounded by their wagon guns which can kill many people at the same time with one shell. Each time, we look at those huge guns and sign their treaties. And each time we do, they break those treaties by taking even more of our land. So what can we do?'

Satanta answered. 'Two summers ago the Americans ended their great war between the North and South in which they slaughtered each other in numbers greater than there are Indians in all this land they called America. Twenty summers before that they invaded Mexico and many more thousands were killed. It seems it is permissible for the blue-coats to kill Texans and Mexicans. But when we raid the people in these same two places they tell us we are wrong. We have always fought the Texans and Mexicans. But we have never fought Americans so why should they worry what we do in Texas and Mexico?

'They have laws for themselves but different laws for Indians. So we have no choice. We must sign the treaty just as they want us to and accept all their presents. Then we can leave their council at Medicine Lodge and do just as they do – break the treaty! After it is signed they will go their own way so we will go ours. Nothing will have changed. Except that it will give us time to plan our next strategies.'

'But we do not know what they want of us,' countered Kicking Bird, a warrior in his early thirties who knew in his heart that the white men would win eventually; for they had the advantages of superior weapons and apparently limitless numbers of cavalry, known to the Indians as pony soldiers. 'Like you, I have no desire to lose more of our land. But we all know that if we do not give it to them, they will take it anyway. And many Kiowas will die. Satank spoke truly when he said we were the smallest nation. We cannot afford to lose many more of our warriors or the Kiowas will no longer exist as a people.'

Satanta spat into the fire and snarled: 'Better to die standing up than to live on our hands and knees! Are we to spend our time in this world grovelling around like dogs at the feet of the Americans? To go to them when we are called? To beg them for even the smallest and poorest pieces of meat?' He stood up and his voice became much louder. 'For that is what it means to live upon a white man's reservation!' he shouted. 'I have seen it happen to other tribes. It must never happen to the Kiowas. If they are to have our land, then so be it. But let it not happen until that same land has been stained forever red by the last drop of Kiowa blood!' Blinded with tears of emotion, Satanta stumbled away into the darkness surrounding the camp.

Smaller arguments broke out among all the council fires but the big meeting was over. Everything important enough to be put into words had been said already. And Satanta had spoken for most of them with his final outburst. But not all. For several Kiowas agreed with Kicking Bird. They had their doubts, as did many who followed Satank and Satanta. But what else was open to them. The choices were obvious. To live within the

15

boundaries of the reservations that would be allotted to them and to attempt to adapt to the white man's way of life. Or to be hunted relentlessly and killed mercilessly like wild animals. It was a terrible choice. But they knew that it had to be made. The split within the tribe was becoming a bridgeless chasm.

# Chapter Two

Members of the Indian Peace Commission who were to meet with the five tribes of the Southern Plains to discuss the proposed peace treaty set out from Fort Larned, Kansas, on October 11 1867 to march the eighty miles that separated them from Medicine Lodge Creek to the south-east, where the Kiowas, Comanches, Southern Cheyennes, Arapahoes and Kiowa-Apaches had already started to gather in their thousands.

It was a most impressive cavalcade that left the fort that day. More than two miles long, the procession consisted of the peace commissioners, Indian agents, distinguished state officials, newspaper correspondents and Major Joel Elliott accompanied by five hundred troopers of the Seventh Cavalry. The latter provided an escort not only for the members of the peace commission but also for almost one hundred wagons crammed with supplies and gifts for the Indians.

For most of the five thousand Southern Indians expected at the peace council, those loaded wagons were their sole reason for attending the meeting at Medicine Lodge. Many of them, like the Kiowas, had ridden distances of five hundred miles and more. Through the searing heat of the Llano Estacado of Texas, the dry dust of the Indian Territory, today known as the state of Oklahoma, to reach by the time specified that part of

17

southern Kansas called Medicine Lodge Creek. Not to make peace with the land-hungry whites – but to make certain that they rode away with their share, and more if possible, of the gifts being brought to the council by the Americans.

The white man's dictum of something for nothing was no longer his prerogative alone. For it was an attitude that the Indians had been both eager and quick to learn. If the Americans were more than enthusiastic to hand over huge amounts of trade goods in exchange for marks made by the Indian chiefs on sheets of printed paper – which neither side intended to honour and which, in most instances, the copper-coloured people of the plains did not even understand – then that was fine by the Indians. For them the Medicine Lodge Treaty ceremony was the mother and father of all such gatherings. There were more than enough gifts for all these happy-go-lucky nomads of the Southern Plains who seldom worried themselves about that obscurity which the whites termed 'tomorrow'.

And what a gathering! Colour, movement, noise, smells, dust and people were in evidence for miles around Medicine Lodge Creek. Indian tepees and army bivouacks gave parts of the area an appearance of semi-permanence. On the surface there seemed to exist the atmosphere of carnival. But not far beneath this surface lurked much hostility which would take but very little to fan its glowing embers into uncontrollable flames.

The Indian chiefs, of the Kiowas and Comanches in particular, were striving desperately to stop their young warriors from openly baiting the soldiers who sat astride their mounts in long rigidly straight lines as if back on the parade ground at Ford Larned. The young men of the tribes present wanted to impress the many young Indian maidens assembled there. For from among these would come the brides of many of these frisky young warriors. These red-skinned fighters wanted to look good. And who could provide them with a better opportunity than their bitter enemies, the blue-coat pony soldiers? They would gallop flat out, lances extended, at the columns of stationary cavalry troopers – only to pull their horses to a sudden, vicious halt at the last possible moment, laughing at the soldiers' obvious discomfort; and then wheel around to go through the same process again and again.

The cavalry officers and sergeants held their men in rigid immobility while the chiefs gradually restrained their own braves. However, there was one solitary incident more dangerous than all the other happenings, which could have ended the peace conference before it had even started but for the strict discipline of the leaders on both sides.

Walks-Like-A-Shadow watched as a beautiful Kiowa girl named Summer Cloud walked slowly, lightly and with dignity in front of the lines of mounted troopers. She had many suitors but he had promised himself that one day soon she would be his wife. In fact, there was but one obstacle which prevented him from being with her at this very moment. He lacked the courage to tell her of his intentions. What a strange world it was, he reflected, in which a brave warrior could be reduced to a quivering hulk by even one look from the woman he loved.

His reverie, however, was brought to an abrupt end as he heard one soldier say to another: 'She might be a red-skin by God; but I'd rather mount her than this brute between my legs right now.' His comrade chuckled. 'I wouldn't mind a go at one or two of those beauties myself,' he said.

Walks-Like-A-Shadow guided his horse across the few paces that separated him from the two troopers. His face was a mask of anger. His hunting knife was in his hand. 'You! Yes, I talk to you pony soldier,' he snarled in English at the one who had spoken first. 'That woman you say things about. She is my woman.' He sliced the air with his knife in a downward cutting motion. 'If you touch her then I cut you one place so you never can have any woman again.'

'You red son-of-a-bitch!' exploded the trooper as he unbuttoned the holster of his side-arm, a regulation .44 Colt revolver. 'I'll blow your damn head off!'

A sergeant rode up quietly from behind him and grabbed his gun hand in a grip of granite. 'Quilter,' hissed the sergeant in little more than a whisper, 'You take your hand away from that pistol or I'll knock your damned head off! Do you hear me boy?'

Quilter nodded. To him all Indians were for sport of one kind or another, but tough sergeants like the massive Ryan towering beside him were a totally different game. A game he did not intend playing because men like Ryan made the rules up as they went along. He withdrew his hand carefully away from his revolver butt and just as carefully rebuttoned his holster.

Equally as fast as the sergeant and just as noiselessly, Satank reined his pony alongside Walks-Like-A-Shadow. 'Put your knife away,' he growled in Kiowa. 'This is no time for private quarrels – particularly with blue-coat soldiers. Do you want our women and children caught in the middle of a blood bath? Because that is what will happen if young hot-heads like you and that pony soldier start fighting each other with weapons.'

Walks-Like-A-Shadow thrust his keen-edged knife back in its sheath and rode off shamefaced. He was so angry that he did not see the gentle eyes of Summer Cloud follow him as he moved away.

But he did hear the pony-soldier chief, Major Elliott, speak to the trooper who had insulted her. 'I heard you Quilter,' he snapped. 'Every filthy word you said. Well, I don't give a damn what trouble your dirty mouth gets you into personally. But I do care when it endangers a whole peace mission. Sergeant Ryan, I want this man placed under close arrest as soon as we get back to the fort.'

'Yes sir!'

The major rode back over to where his fellow officers, the chiefs of the five tribes, members of the peace commission, state officials, Indian agents and newspaper reporters were all waiting impatiently for the treaty talks to commence.

There had been so many such treaty meetings between the Southern Plains Indians and the Americans in the past that the procedure they now followed had become virtually a ritual. Although the Indians present did not know it at the time, this was to be the last occasion when they would participate in such tragicomic charades. For the commissioners had been informed by Congress that this was to be a final attempt at securing a lasting peace with the Southern Plains tribes. Congress had sent out an investigative commission the previous year to determine the causes behind the perpetual breakdowns in all previous treaties with these southern Indians. The reports they received from the investigators had an all too familiar sound to them. Due to the greed and corruption of American businessmen, politicians and Indian agents, the annuity goods promised to these people of the Southern Plains during earlier treaties were always of the shoddiest quality when they were eventually delivered and were of no use whatever to the red men. So the warriors of these tribes immediatedly recommenced raiding Texan and Mexican settlements in order to make good all resultant deficiencies. This apart, they enjoyed raiding into Mexico and Texas just as they had for countless years past.

So this meeting, as with all those before it, conformed to what was now the expected pattern. The peace commissioners with their large retinue and even larger escort of soldiers clad in their dress uniforms. And the numerous chiefs with their thousands of warriors daubed with traditional markings in gaudy paints which had taken many hours to prepare. Field kitchens set up in strategic positions throughout the council ground by the army's catering department so that there would be plentiful supplies of food and coffee to help prevent any unnecessary interruptions in the business about to be transacted.

At last the treaty council was under way. Gifts were exchanged between both sides. Then, finally, the commissioners, officers, interpreters and chiefs all seated themselves in a circle surrounded by the thousands of other people present. The traditional Indian pipe of peace was passed around the circle in absolute silence so that all seated there could take one puff at the pipe to show that everything was well before the serious part of the proceedings started.

The first to speak were the Americans. The leader of

the peace commission stood up. 'Your big white father in Washington has . . .'

'My father not big, not white and not in Washington!' shouted a warrior in passable English from somewhere deep in the crowd around the circle. 'He very little, very brown and he beside me now.'

There was a great roar of laughter, particularly from the white soldiers who obviously could appreciate a joke in English far better than most of the Indians present.

The embarrassed commissioner waited for the laughter to subside before continuing. 'He has asked me to tell all the tribes of the Southern Plains that they will be given areas of land far distant from all American travel routes and settlements so that there will be no more fighting between our peoples. You will also be supplied with foodstuffs, seeds and farm implements. Instructors will be sent to you to show you how to make farms of your own just as the white men do.

'You will be given tools as well and shown how to build houses fit to live in. Houses that will shade you from the heat of the sun in summer and protect you from the rain, winds and snow in winter. Schools will be built for you by the big father in . . . by the people sent out to you by the President in Washington. You will also be provided with a doctor to help you when you are sick. And annual allocations of clothing and other items necessary for your welfare will be made to you for the next thirty years.

'All that is asked of you in return by our government in Washington is that from the moment this new treaty is signed you will stop forever all wars against the whites and cease interfering with the construction upon your lands of forts, roads and rails.'

As his words were translated for the benefit of the chiefs, many angry mutterings were heard from among the members of the five tribes gathered around them.

The leader of the peace commission pressed on. 'The white government loves its red brothers but you must also remember how great are its powers. You have all behaved badly by breaking past treaties. In fact, some of your young braves are raiding in Texas, Mexico and parts of Kansas even as I speak.

'But not all the wrongs which have resulted in broken treaties have been carried out by Indians. We all know this. We know that there are some white men who have treated you badly. That is why we are here. I have spoken the words of Washington. Now it is up to you to tell your side of all these matters.'

Slowly and painfully, an elderly but much respected Comanche chief rose to his feet with great dignity of bearing. He walked steadily to the centre of the circle. His name was Par-roowah Sermehno, known to the Americans and history as Ten Bears. He was one of the most capable of all Indian orators to be found anywhere in the vast American West.

His words were simple but intelligent. Sometimes logical and, at other times, illogical. To most of the white men assembled there his arguments were those of a man who was unable to see far into the future. But, whatever their limitations, his words were the views of his people and he was putting them across as only Ten Bears knew how.

'My heart is filled with joy when I see you here. My people have never first drawn a bow or fired a gun against the whites. There has been trouble between us. My young men have danced the war dance. But it was not begun by us. It was you who sent out the first soldier.

'You said you wanted to put us on a reservation, to build us houses and makes us medicine lodges (churches). I do not want them. I was born upon the prairie where the wind blew free and there was nothing to break the light of the sun. I was born where there were no enclosures, and where everything drew a free breath. I want to die there and not within walls. I know every stream and every wood between the Rio Grande and the Arkansas. I have hunted and lived over the country. I lived like my fathers before me, and, like them, I have lived happily.

'When I was at Washington the Great Father told me that all of the Comanche land was ours, and that no one should hinder us in living upon it. So, why do you ask us to leave the rivers, and the sun, and the wind, and live in houses? Do not speak of it any more. I love to carry out the talk I get from the Great Father. When I get goods and presents I and my people feel glad, since it shows that he holds us in his eye. If the Texans had been kept out of my country, there might have been peace. The white man has the country we loved, and we only wish to wander on the prairie until we die. I want no blood upon my land to stain the grass.'

There were many audible murmurs of approval as Ten Bears returned slowly to his place and sat down. Even the aged Satank nodded his head in acknowledgement of the wisdom of Ten Bear's words.

But it was Satanta who spoke on behalf of the Kiowa people. 'All the land south of the Arkansas River belongs to the Kiowas and Comanches, and I do not want to give any of it away. I love the land and the buffalo and will not part with it. I do not want any of the medicine lodges

25

within my country. I want the children raised as I was. I have heard that you want to settle us on a reservation near the mountains. I do not want to settle. I love to roam over the prairies. There I feel free and happy; but when I settle down I grow pale and die. A long time ago this land belonged to our fathers; but when I go up the river I see camps of soldiers on its banks. These soldiers cut down my timber; they kill my buffalo; and when I see that, it feels as if my head would burst with sorrow.'

As the soldiers listened to his arguments, the buzz of agreement grew louder. Walks-Like-A-shadow turned to his best friend, Bull Shoulders, so-called because of his massive build and, like his comrade, also a member of the Crazy Horses military society. 'Is not Satanta the greatest talker of them all,' said Walks-Like-A-Shadow, not as a question but as a statement of fact.

'He is so, my friend,' agreed Bull Shoulders. 'And it looks as if he has more to say.'

Bull Shoulders was right because Satanta continued: 'This building of homes for us is all nonsense. We do not want you to build any for us; we would all die. Look at the Penatekas! Once they were a powerful tribe, but now they are weak and poor. I want all my land, even from the Arkansas River south to the Red River. My country is small enough already. If you build us houses the land will be smaller. Why do you insist on this? What good will come of it? I do not understand your reasons. Time enough to build us houses when the buffalo are all gone. But you tell the Great Father that there are plenty of buffalo yet; and when the buffalo are gone, I will tell him so. This trusting to agents for food I do not believe in.'

There were other speakers, such as Little Raven of the

Arapahoes, but it was the words of Satanta which left the members of the Indian Peace Commission most disturbed and confused. They had anticipated little, if any, opposition from the Indians. They had expected such formalities as the exchanging of gifts and the making of speeches – but not this blunt rejection of all their carefully planned proposals.

To such men as the peace commissioners, civilizing the red man was something which could be accomplished overnight. You impressed him with a display of your strength, told him what you expected of him, let him say a few words in formal reply, then thrust into his hands a spade, rake, or hoe and you had a ready-made farmer. Were Indians not creatures of the land? Then why did they not wish to become farmers? Why did they not want to live in permanent houses? It was ridiculous. You could not civilize nomads.

They could not believe that the red men did not need, or even desire, all the so-called advantages of so-called civilised society. It was ludicrous that the Indians required nothing other than what they had. And of all the enticements offered them, it was apparent that the one thing they wanted least of all was any form of assistance or, as the red men termed it, interference, from the American people. And they expected the government to permit them to continue raiding settlements in Texas and Mexico. It was outrageous! It was scandalous! Whose land was it anyway?

Suddenly, Many Kills, a powerful and warlike sub chief of the Kiowas with a strong following among the younger warriors, stood up and shouted at the commissioners. 'Are you blind?' he almost screamed at them. 'Can you not see? We do not want your way of life! We do not want your gifts! For they are not gifts no matter what you would have us believe. Because, in the end, we always have to pay a price for them. And the price is always far beyond their worth.

'Eighteen summers ago (1849) some white men discovered a useless yellow metal, which you call gold, to the west of our land. You cannot make utensils or weapons from this metal. It has none of the uses of iron. But Americans value it above all other metals. It drives them crazy. They burrow into the ground like wild animals to get at it. They even kill each other for it. They crossed our land in countless thousands to reach the place you call California. In those days the Kiowas and Comanches also had countless thousands of people. But those crazy Americans gave us a big gift as they crossed our land. They gave us cholera. And now, as a result of that epidemic, the Kiowas and Comanches are less than three thousand in number together. No, we do not want your ways or your gifts!' And with these words Many Kills strode from the council meeting. Many of the younger braves followed him.

But it was to no avail. The walk-out was an empty gesture – nothing more. As usual the American government had its way. The Medicine Lodge Treaty was signed soon after by all five tribes. The Kiowas and Comanches were talked into accepting the treaty ten days later, on October 21. Later that same day the Kiowa-Apaches also signed. The Arapahoes and Southern Cheyennes capitulated a week later, on October 28.

# Chapter Three

Congress debated the Medicine Lodge Treaty at considerable length. Winter had arrived and it was no longer 1867 but 1868. The five tribes were cold and hungry. While the Senate and the House, with satisfied stomachs and drowsily warm bodies, disagreed half-heartedly about various aspects of the treaty they were supposed to be ratifying, so the Indians became increasingly restless.

The American officials on the spot could see that the situation among the hostiles was worsening steadily as each day passed without any positive news from Congress. They were extremely worried by this apparent lack of urgency among their superiors in Washington. And, with good reason, they began to fear that even if there was ratification of the treaty it might arrive too late to cool the anger of the thousands of copper-coloured warriors from the Southern Plains. The signs were ominous. The tidal wave of Indian resentment would soon burst through the flimsy dam of peace, constructed by the American commissioners and the tribal leaders, if the gathering storm ever broke with all the fury of which it was capable.

The storm broke on January 5, 1868. On that day an influential Kiowa war leader, Heap-of-Bears, decided to lead a powerful band of marauding warriors into Denton County. In one lightning strike they killed eight Americans and kidnapped two white women and eight children. A posse gave chase but succeeded only in recovering the two women at the expense of one child killed. The Kiowas, together with the remaining seven white youngsters, easily outrode and eluded their pursuers.

The dam now burst completely. February saw roving bands of hostile Kiowas, under such noted leaders as Lone Wolf, Timbered Mountain and Big Bow, swarming into Texas to kill, scalp, kidnap, rape, plunder and torture. Torture rites were an integral part of most Indian cultures. And the Kiowas were known to be the most ingenious torturers of all. It was a reputation that was well earned.

Parties of Texans brave enough to follow any of the raiding parties, in desperate attempts to recover loved ones captured by these savages, were sickened by the trails left by the Kiowas. Young girls had been ripped open and left to die in unbelievable agonies. In other cases captives had been bound to stakes and left facing the sun – with their eyelids cut away. And still the gruesome trail led its stomach-churned trackers on to scenes of even greater horror, with each cameo of sadism more grisly than the one preceding it. The paths the Americans posses followed were both long and bloody. And, in some instances, virtually endless, for the Kiowas were the farthest-ranging marauders of all the Plains Indians.

Another frontier hazard for Texans and Mexicans was the lasting alliance between the Kiowas and Comanches. Since just prior to 1800 these two nations had joined together in a mutual defence pact to protect themselves from the persistent onslaught of much larger plains

tribes. The alliance had been a successful one. So successful, in fact, that it had been but a simple, natural and
irresistible transition from the miserable role of victim
to the much grander, and far more rewarding, one of
predator. The favourite stages upon which the combined
talents of these two warrior peoples were displayed
to their greatest advantage were scattered throughout
many parts of Mexico and Texas. But the former was
the more favoured by both Kiowas and Comanches; the
merest mention of whose names was sufficient to cause
most Mexicans to cross themselves and look anxiously
around for the most convenient place of concealment –
just in case!

Their fears, and those of their Texan neighbours, were
soon justified for it was not long before the Comanches
were also making successful forays across the borders
into these two territories. It was the old story repeated
yet again. The Southern Plains wept while Washington
slept!

These raids continued throughout the spring and into
the summer. But one warrior was absent from them all.
Not because he disagreed with them. Neither was he at
all afraid. It was simply that Walks-Like-A-Shadow had
other things in mind. Well, just one person in mind to
be precise – Summer Cloud.

Spring can make a young warrior restless for things
other than the war-path. And, unlike other springs
that had gone before, Walks-Like-A-Shadow had few
thoughts this year which did not include Summer Cloud
in some way. Wherever she was, then he was close by.
The women of the village noticed; and giggled. Those
men who were not away raiding also saw – but they
merely grinned knowingly. If Walks-Like-A-Shadow

preferred looking at a woman to fighting then he really was ready for marriage. Or so they thought.

Only Walks-Like-A-Shadow, and perhaps Summer Cloud, had any doubts. For the young warrior had not yet entered into the customary bargaining with her parents.

'Why am I not doing so?' he asked himself as he watched her washing clothes in a stream one April morning.

'Why is he not doing so?' she asked herself as she scrubbed at the clothes half-heartedly, sensing that Walks-Like-A-Shadow was not far away.

'Is she not the most beautiful woman I have ever seen?' As he watched, her long black hair, with its blue metallic sheen, fell across her face. She brushed it away from her almost perfect features with both hands before continuing with the washing. She had the high cheekbones of other Kiowa women but her face was not wide like theirs. It was narrower, with gentle brown eyes, a slightly upturned nose, full lips and teeth that sparkled in the morning sun like virgin snow.

He knew that he wanted this woman for all time. His heart pounded for her. His eyes desired her. And his body ached for her. But he did not want her to become his wife just because the price he offered her parents was sufficiently high. She had many admirers and he was wealthy enough to outbid them all. No, if this woman was to be his then it must be because she so desired it just as he did. There could be no other way. This thing he knew. But within the Kiowa society, to find out the true feelings of such a woman as Summer Cloud would be an extremely difficult task for young unmarried women were never without their chaperones. And even as he watched her closely, from amidst the saplings of a nearby thicket, so did her well-rounded mother, seated solidly on a large boulder a few paces behind her daughter.

How could he move that vigilant mountain of flesh for sufficient time in which to speak to her beautiful daughter? Suddenly he grinned to himself and slipped noiselessly away into the surrounding brush.

Minutes later he reappeared at the entrance to their tepee which was situated within easy access of the stream so that Summer Cloud's mother did not have to walk – or, rather waddle – too far to obtain water. In the young warrior's hands were green twigs and leaves he had broken from the bushes just before emerging into the open. He made certain that no one saw him as he entered their tepee. Once inside he used the twigs and leaves to create a fire in the centre of the family lodge – the father was away hunting – which would cause no damage but which would send great clouds of smoke billowing forth.

'That should allow me to get her away from her mother for time enough,' he mused as he crept unseen from the tepee.

Suddenly the morning stillness was shattered by cries of 'Fire! Fire!'

Both Summer Cloud and her mother turned towards the village. 'Ai-yee!' sreamed the suddenly motivated mountain. 'It is our lodge daughter. Quickly!' And, with an agility so unbelievable in one of such immense girth that it left Walks-Like-A-Shadow temporarily stunned, she bounced towards the smoking tepee like a gigantic mobile sack of prairie onions.

So amazed at the apparition that bundled past him as he stood hidden amidst the tall saplings at the edge of the thicket, Walks-Like-A-Shadow almost forgot what he had set out to accomplish. For Summer Cloud almost passed him also as she chased after her mother. But not quite. For he recovered his senses just in time to seize her and pull her into the thicket with him. Her cry of astonishment was lost amidst the uproar going on around them. Walks-Like-A-Shadow put one hand firmly but gently across her mouth to stifle any further screams as he held her securely with his other arm. She struggled. But only briefly. For her protests, both verbal and physical, froze within her trembling young body immediatedly she realised who was holding her.

'Well, woman, will you remain quiet if I take my hand from your mouth?' demanded her captor.

She nodded. Walks-Like-A-Shadow removed both hands and allowed her to stand free. She was still shaking.

'Are you cold that you tremble so, or do I frighten you that much?' he asked. But the sharp edge had gone from his voice.

'It is neither,' she mumbled in reply, 'Although you did surprise me greatly.'

'Well?'

'Well what?'

'Are you going to run off now that I have set you loose?'

'If you wish me to run from you then why did you grab hold of me in the first place?' she asked in feigned innocence. Summer Cloud had rapidly recovered her composure and was now enjoying the other's obvious discomfort. There was a look of mischief upon her features that anyone, other than a lovesick young man, would soon have noticed.

But Walks-Like-A-Shadow was a lovesick young man so he noticed not. He was acutely embarrassed. This was not at all what he had anticipated. In fact, now that it was too late, he had not even considered in advance what reaction to expect of her. The heat of the moment had not permitted his thoughts to go any further than the act. Well, here she was and he was a speechless fool.

'Well,' she repeated, 'Do you wish me to run away?' Summer Cloud made as if to move off.

Walks-Like-A-Shadow recovered his voice. 'No. Stay with me . . . please.' His words came low and husky from the nervousness within him. 'Please stay. Even if only for a few moments.'

'Is that all you want me for – just a few moments?' she teased.

He hesitated. 'I am not sure how to say it,' he whispered hoarsely. 'For I have not once felt this way before. It is all so new to me and I am lost like a small boy in a large forest that he has never before entered.'

'Then I will make it easy for you because it is evident that we both feel this same thing.' There was no mischief in her voice this time. Instead, in its place, there was a gentle seriousness. 'How long do you wish me to stay with Walks-Like-A-Shadow?' she asked.

His heart almost beat its way through his chest as he heard her words; and the sound of his name upon her tongue was like a strange music to his ears. 'For all my life upon this earth,' he replied simply.

'That is what I have heard you say so many times in my dreams.' And she moved closer to him.

The smell of her body as she stood in front of him made him reach out and pull her closely to him. Then the sensation, as she did not resist but rubbed her entire length against him, transferred itself from his arms into his loins. He had never known such exquisite agony.

'You are thinking with parts of your body other than your head,' she teased him tenderly. 'I can even feel your thoughts.'

'I am ... sorry,' he blurted out in embarrassment, drawing back from her.

She moved her body close against his as before. 'Do not be sorry,' she whispered. 'I too feel this way. But a woman's desires are not so obvious as those of a man. There is nothing wrong with such thoughts. They are a most natural thing between two people in love.'

'Then you are not angry with me Summer Cloud?'

'Of course not,' she replied. 'But there is one thing.'

'And what is that?' queried Walks-Like-A-Shadow.

'They must remain just thoughts until we are married,' she answered. 'Then we can turn these thoughts into reality.'

This new power within him felt as if it was on the verge of eruption so he pushed her gently from him. 'It is agreed,' he said.

'What is agreed?' demanded a voice from close by, which made them both leap apart as if they had suddenly found themselves walking upon live coals. It was Summer Cloud's mother.

Walks-Like-A-Shadow found his mouth unexpectedly dry. He opened it but no words came out.

'Are you struck dumb or was that not your voice I heard just now telling my daughter that it was agreed? Whatever it may be.'

The young warrior managed to control his tongue and force it to speak again. But the words he uttered were not in answer to her question. 'How did you get close without us hearing?' His eyes clearly displayed the disbelief of the mind behind them.

'Oh, I am well aware of my size without any reminders from you,' retorted Summer Cloud's mother. 'But I was not always this large. It came when giving birth to that young maiden you were embracing but a short time ago. You are a big man but are called Walks-Like-A-Shadow. So do not be surprised when I tell you that I am named Walks-Like-A-Feather. The size does not matter, do you agree?'

He could only nod as she continued: 'Neither am I as green as the wood you used to start the fire in our lodge in order to divert my attention.'

'How did you know?' gasped Walks-Like-A-Shadow in amazement.

'If a woman loses her figure, as I did all those years back, then she must develop other ways of keeping her man if she loves him. I learned to cook like no other woman can and I taught myself to anticipate my husband's wishes before he even puts them into words. Your ploy was not clever enough to outsmart me for long. And I knew who was responsible for it when my daughter was no longer with me for I have seen the way you look at one another. No, it was simply a matter of finding you.'

'Which you did,' said Walks-Like-A-Shadow in open-mouthed admiration. 'It is truly incredible. You should have been born a boy. What a warrior you would have made. Nobody has ever caught me like this before.'

'With my daughter? I should hope not!'

The young warrior was flustered once more. 'No, that is not what I meant. I . . . I . . . I . . . that is . . . I . . .' he stuttered helplessly.

'I think you had better stop there for you have almost as many "eyes" as a spider.' Suddenly her massive frame started shuddering with silent laughter. 'I am only teasing,' she said, brushing the tears from her eyes with the back of her hand. 'From whom do you think Summer Cloud inherited her sense of humour? Certainly not from her father – as you will soon learn when you start courting our daughter in the proper manner instead of by starting fires. A fire in her heart I will accept but not another one in our tepee! Is that understood?'

Walks-Like-A-Shadow could only nod in agreement at the clever words of this remarkable woman. But Summer Cloud heard not only her mother's words but understood immediately the meaning of them. 'So you agree to the marriage?' she gasped.

'Of course I do. It is obvious you are for each other and no one else.' She looked at the anxiety etched clearly upon the features of her daughter's young suitor. 'Do not worry,' she told him. 'Her father may not have a sense of humour. Neither does he have any sense where the women of his family are concerned. Between us we always get him to do as we wish, do we not daughter?'

'Yes, it has always been so. He has never once been able to refuse you. And I have learned well from you.' Summer Cloud's eyes were filled with happiness as she spoke.

Several weeks later she was married to Walks-Like-A-Shadow.

# Chapter Four

In July of 1868, not long after his marriage to Summer Cloud, Walks-Like-A-Shadow was one of several thousand angry Kiowa and Comanche warriors congregated at Port Larned. They were there to collect their annuity goods as promised by the peace commission during the treaty talks at Medicine Lodge. That they were in a turbulent mood was due to the fact that the goods had not arrived. They had been delayed by transportation difficulties and were still in the depot at Lawrence, Kansas. But the officers at Fort Larned could not argue such fine points with vast hordes of Indian fighting men made even less amenable to reasoning by the consumption of countless gallons of so-called whisky sold to them by unscrupulous, money-grabbing white liquor dealers.

It was a hard fact of life that no Indian could hold his whisky like a white man. It took very little liquor to get a red man drunk. He also became addicted to alcohol far quicker than did his white brother. And his white brother soon found it was a great deal easier, and safer, to steal from a broken-down, alcohol-addicted, drunken Indian than it was from a battle seasoned warrior who, stone cold sober, was more than a match, man to man, for any American. Even in many cases where such white men had vastly superior weapons.

So the United States Army continued to improve its

quality of arms. And the frontier ruffians continued to make and sell their deadly brew concocted of raw alcohol, river water, chunks of tobacco and red peppers. The alcohol was the ingredient which provided the stupefaction so many disillusioned Indians sought so readily. The water diluted it sufficiently to keep the copper-coloured customers on their feet long enough to continue buying until their money ran out. The tobacco gave it the required pale brown tint. And the peppers provided the necessary sting and also served to disguise the unwholesome flavours of the other ingredients. Its popular names of 'poison' or 'rotgut', passed on to the better quality whiskies in the saloons of so many frontier towns, were only mild jokes among those who used such terms. But to the Indians who drank the real 'poison' it was no joke. For they died in their thousands of what was, literally, 'rotgut'.

But, before their eventual deaths from the rotgut poisoning, those Indians who drank it regularly – as well as those who consumed it only occasionally – became easily troublesome. Quick to take offence and almost impossible to placate once they were angered, such warriors reverted to the savagery of their ancestors and rapidly turned into murderers, rapists and looters without any real reason. Only the imagined insults stimulated by their consumption of alcohol.

Such was the case in the early hours of the morning of Sunday, July 9, when two intoxicated young Kiowa warriors, astride a solitary horse, galloped headlong through an American camp, screaming as loudly as they could to terrify the white men. But the Americans were not amused. In panic, they tumbled from their beds and fired a volley of shots into the darkness towards the yells

40

of the cavorting warriors. Inevitably, one of the Indians was soon seriously wounded.

The surviving warrior galloped back to the Kiowa camp with his wounded comrade clinging desperately to him. As soon as they were reasonably safe among their fellow braves they swore they had both been fired upon without reason. A war party, many of its members also suffering from the ill effects of bad whisky, was soon on its way to Fort Larned. An unfortunate Mexican who happened to be passing the same way was shot at by the Indians and wounded.

Once they reached the fort, open warfare was averted only by the timely arrival of Satanta who was forced to use all his great persuasive powers of oratory to calm down his drink-crazed tribesmen.

But it was only a brief respite. For later that same day a government wagonmaster galloped into the post, reined his dusty, worn-out mount to a halt on the parade ground and threw himself from the saddle. He strode towards the officers' quarters. 'Where the hell is everyone?' he shouted. 'My whole damn train has been ambushed by a pile of drunken Indians. Goddam it, can't you hear me? Get some goddam soldiers out there fast if you want your rations. Last time I saw 'em those red hellions was busy unloadin' all the coffee, sugar and flour they could carry. For Christ's sake, get a move on!'

An elderly captain of cavalry, pulling on his jacket as he ran, caught up with the wagonmaster from behind. 'Calm down man. Don't get your britches in a twist. What Indians were they? And where in the hell is "out there" may I ask?'

The wagonmaster stopped in his tracks. 'They was Kiowas,' he replied breathlessly, 'And, mister, "out there" right now is anywhere those red sons-of-bitches want it to be! Now all your soldier boys has gotta do is go "out there" and find them – that is if you want your rations!' And he stormed over to the sutler's shop for a stiff drink or two.

A squadron of cavalry and a detachment of infantry were soon in the field searching for the Kiowa raiders. They headed straight for the Kiowa camp on the Arkansas. Several Kiowas were standing by the fort's gate as the soldiers moved off. Among the Indian onlookers was Walks-Like-A-Shadow. He had seen the wagonmaster ride in, he had watched while the man exchanged words with the grizzled captain and now he saw the pony soldiers and foot soldiers marching in the direction of the village of his people.

The young warrior streaked through the open gates shouting in English: 'Where is grey-hair captain? I want speak with captain old-man!'

Several soldiers tried to stop him but he was far too swift for them. He also ran a zig-zag course so that shooting at him would be impossible for fear of shooting one another. Nevertheless, one private raised his carbine and tried to level it at the sprinting Kiowa.

A hand reached across from behind him and firmly pushed down the muzzle of his rifle. It was the same veteran captain for whom Walks-Like-A-Shadow was looking. 'Put that bloody weapon down man,' he hissed at the private. 'Can't you see he's unarmed. Anyway, I think it's me he wants; though lord knows why.'

He looked across at the running warrior and bellowed: 'Hey you!' Walks-Like-A-Shadow glanced over his shoulder to look at the man who had shouted. 'Yes, you Kiowa! Over here!' The warrior turned and ran across to the captain. He stopped in front of the officer, shoulders and chest heaving with exertion and sweat pouring down superbly proportioned muscles.

'Well young man,' said the captain in a surprisingly mild tone, 'What can I do for you? It's obvious you speak some English at least.'

'Yes, I speak your tongue pretty good,' gasped the still panting warrior. 'I see soldiers, many soldiers, go towards village of my people. Why? They got many guns as if want to shoot Kiowas. Why?'

'You saw that man ride through the gates and speak to me?' asked the captain.

'Yes, I see.'

'Well he told me that Kiowa warriors had attacked his wagon train and had stolen goods intended for this post. So I have sent out the soldiers to get back those stolen goods.'

'How you know goods stolen?' queried Walks-Like-A-Shadow.

'Because the wagonmaster told me so,' replied the officer.

'But he not look like man who been in fight,' protested the young Kiowa warrior. 'He no wounded. Clothes not torn. Only dusty. Horse not harmed. Him fightened man but not been in fight with Kiowas. This thing I know for sure because I know my warrior brothers.'

The veteran army captain stared straight into the eyes of the young Indian. Unflinching, the Kiowa brave stared rigidly back at the elderly officer. Then, abruptly and without warning, the captain barked: 'Sergeant Ryan!'

Running footsteps, clicking heels, a quick salute and 'Yessir!'

'Sergeant I want you to have a few words with our

43

wagonmaster friend – unofficially of course. I want to know if there really was a raid on his wagons. And I want the truth. How you get it, I leave to your own discretion. But I want the truth. It's an unofficial request so you can refuse if you've a mind. Well?'

'Yessir. I'll do it. Unofficial of course.' There was a gleam in the sergeant's eyes. 'That bastard cheated me out of a month's pay at cards a while back. It'll be a pleasure sir.' He saluted, turned and marched off. Twenty minutes later he was back. There were smears of blood on his knuckles as he saluted.

'Captain Jarvis sir! Sergeant Ryan reporting with information as requested sir. Unofficially of course,' he said with a wide, worldly grin.

'Well, sergeant?'

'It would appear sir that there was no raid at all. Some drunken Kiowas surrounded his wagons asking for their annuity goods which they thought were in the wagons. The wagon boss panics and starts throwing them anything and everything. Then he tells them to take what they wants. Then, while their backs is turned, he hightails it here to the fort shouting bloody blue murder about being raided. He knew the army would have fired him if the truth was known.'

'And he would have been willing to start a real killing war to save his job,' mused Captain Jarvis.

'Yessir. That he would,' returned the sergeant.

'And he still will if we don't stop it right now,' barked the captain, suddenly snapping into action.

'Sergeant, you and this Kiowa here can easily outride cavalry slowed down by infantry if you cut across country. Well, can't you?'

'Shouldn't be too hard sir.'

'Damn it, what are you waiting for man?'

'Your orders sir.'

'Well, you've got them,' came the reply, 'So get to it!'

'What about a horse for the Kiowa sir? Mine's ready and waiting.'

'Give him mine blast it; but move your cantankerous hide.'

Sergeant Ryan beckoned to Walks-Like-A-Shadow who had understood most of what had passed between the two army men. Within minutes the sergeant and the Kiowa were streaking on horseback through the gates of Fort Larned and flat out across the surrounding prairie. Two fighting men, one white and the other red, hell-bent on stopping a war between the United States Army and the Kiowa nation.

And they only just made it. For as the two men reined their lathered mounts to a halt between the two factions, both sides were squaring up to each other. Frightened Kiowa women and children, covered by the warriors of the tribe, were already swimming across the river to the comparative safety of the far bank.

'Well, Kiowa, me lad, we made it,' grinned Ryan.

'Yes sergeant. We stopped trouble. I no forget you and captain. My people owe you much.'

Sergeant Ryan turned towards Walks-Like-A-Shadow and there was now a serious edge to his voice. 'No, whatever your name is, you owe us nothing. In fact we owe you because you stopped the captain, who I admire greatly, from being made to look a fool and maybe being kicked out the army without a pension.

'Perhaps I can pay back a little of what we owe by telling you that Quilter, the soldier you almost fought with at Medicine Lodge, escaped from custody on the way back to Fort Larned. He's sworn to kill you boy. And he will unless we get to him first. But I doubt we will. He's cagey and it's one helluva big country. So watch your back. I've warned you. It ain't much, but at least you know your enemy. And that might help some.'

'Thank you sergeant,' replied Walks-Like-A-Shadow, 'And I think I know new friends also. May we never meet in field of battle. It is easy kill enemy. Very hard kill friend. I hope it never happen you and me.'

'Me too son,' the sergeant agreed quietly, almost to himself, as Walks-Like-A-Shadow dismounted and handed him the reins of the captain's horse. 'By the way my name's Ryan. What's yours?'

'I am called Walks-Like-A-Shadow,' came the reply as the bronzed young warrior loped away on foot through the long prairie grass.

The sergeant's eyes followed the fleet-footed runner until his outline disappeared into the hazy distance where the sky merged with the earth. Then he looked away and urged his horse forward with a few softly spoken words. He was surprised to find that his eyes were misty and that there was a huskiness in his voice.

In the meantime the so-called assault upon the supply wagons had been reported to Brigadier General Alfred Sully who commanded the District of the Arkansas, which incorporated Fort Larned. He arrived at the supposedly threatened post with reinforcements of eight companies of the Seventh Cavalry. However, all was quiet at the fort as they rode in. The thousands of Indians gathered there were still hungry but they seemed peaceful enough. When questioned by the general, the many chiefs present blamed the sporadic outbreaks by their young men as directly attributable to the unscrupulous

American whisky dealers. But they also admitted that their young warriors were becoming increasingly difficult to control. At times, in fact, it was impossible to hold them in check at all, the chiefs told the general.

Assessing the situation far quicker than his stagnant-minded superiors in Washington, and with much greater accuracy, General Sully came to the immediate conclusion that unless the people of the five southern tribes were issued with food at once then there would be widespread warfare. 'It's a damn sight cheaper and easier to feed them than it is to fight them,' he commented to his junior officers as he arranged for a separate delivery of goods to be made to the Kiowas and Comanches without delay.

But when the promised food and other items necessary to see the Indians through the approaching winter finally arrived it was the usual case of much too little and far too late. So, as a result, many of those Indians who had waited patiently for the supplies, stoically gathered together their pathetic little bundles of belongings and headed away from the fort towards their normal winter camping grounds scattered throughout the seemingly endless grasslands to the south.

Those warriors who had remained behind now rode headlong towards Texas and Mexico, through which their less patient comrades had already been marauding for some weeks now, in order to obtain sufficient supplies to sustain their families during the long cold months ahead. Winter was ever a tough time on the plains. For the tribes who inhabited them it meant an almost perpetual struggle, month after month, against weather which never conceded a solitary inch that it did not intend so to give. The weakest Indians, no matter what their ages, rarely lived into spring. Winter always held the land tightly within its icy, iron-hard grip until the last possible moment. And it never failed to gather its share of victims before moving on and permitting the long-awaited warmer weather to take its place each year.

To make the situation even harsher for the plains people, the cruel winter would have an equally ruthless ally this year – the United States Army. The army's top brass had decided to mount a winter campaign against the five southern tribes. Indian ponies fed on grass, not upon grain as did U.S. cavalry mounts, so raiding was normally confined to the warmer months when their staple diet was not covered by thick layers of snow and ice. Winter was a time when the tribes stayed within their villages and people sat around the fires in the comfort of their lodges; telling of thrilling exploits of the past and planning equally daring actions for the future. What better time to hit them – and hit them harder than ever they had known before – reasoned the American generals. Kill them as they slept; so to speak. There would not be enough of them left for even a minor spring foray the next year, boasted the army officers in the comparative comfort of their quarters and mess rooms.

But it was a vast and rugged country that favoured white soldiers no more than it did their red counterparts. It was an easy country in which to become lost – and people who did so were soon devoured by the ravenous appetite of winter. However, after lengthy and repetitive discussions, the brass-hats decided that the proposed scheme displayed far more positive features than it did negative aspects. So, the gigantic snow spectacular was approved.

The five southern tribes were divided into two factions

– the guilty and the innocent – by their white judges at a trial attended by no red man and about which no Indian had even the slightest knowledge. General William T. Sherman and Philip H. Sheridan had already decided that the depredations of that summer had been committed mainly by the Arapahoes and Southern Cheyennes so the winter war would be waged against these two tribes.

If these tribes were the guilty ones then it was obvious to the two generals that, by whatever reasoning they had employed to come to this conclusion, the remaining three – the Kiowas, Comanches and Kiowa-Apaches – as a result, must be innocent.

Accordingly, Brigadier General William B. Hazen was instructed to see that these three tribes were tucked safely within the secure environs of Fort Cobb in Indian Territory so that they would not be harmed during the forthcoming winter hostilities. With the peoples of the three tribes concerned scattered over thousands of square miles of crudely mapped territiory, Brigadier General Hazen was entitled to wear the bewildered and worried look that appeared upon his face immediately he heard the orders of his two superiors.

Late in September, however, he was able to arrange a meeting of General Sheridan with most of the Kiowa chiefs and also Ten Bears, of the Comanches. Walks-Like-A-Shadow was there as interpreter.

'Chief Satanta say where this place you call Fort Cobb?' asked Walks-Like-A-Shadow.

'On the Washita River in Indian Territory,' replied Sheridan.

'Chief say no heard of these names, so how far Fort Cobb?'

'About two hundred and twenty miles almost due south of Fort Larned – as the eagle flies – tell your chief.'

'Satanta say too damn far and he no damn eagle!'

'You tell him he has no choice!' snapped Sheridan. 'General Hazen will lead him and his people and the Comanches to the reservation at Fort Cobb. I have ordered enough rations for all your people for this journey. However, as it will take about ten days to get the necessary supplies together, tell the chiefs that I suggest that they use this time to hunt buffalo so that they can supplement their food rations with fresh or cured meat.' Without waiting for a reply, and in order not to allow any further argument on the subject, General Sheridan turned abruptly away and strode rapidly over to where a group of officers stood, lounged or sat in conversation.

Within a short time Satanta had left the area to go on the buffalo hunt. He was accompanied by Walks-Like-A-Shadow, Bull Shoulders and many other stalwart braves. Soon the remaining Indians began slipping away; at first individually, then in families and, before long, in whole groups. It was all accomplished so smoothly and quietly that the military was not aware that they had gone until there were no more Indians left in the vicinity.

The generals sweated! They feared that these doughty warriors of the Kiowas, Comanches and Kiowa-Apaches had joined the Arapahoes and the Southern Cheyennes in the war between red and white which was now raging throughout the plains of the south. When the ten days were up and none of them returned from the buffalo hunt, the generals were certain, in their own minds at least, that all five tribes were now on the war-path.

'Christ, if they are then we are in for one hell of a winter,' Sheridan grumbled to Hazen. 'Texas will be one mass of blood and flames. Why, in God's name, can't these savages fight a stand-up battle instead of all these hit and run raids? You watch, Hazen, and see if I'm not right. They'll send dozens of small parties out and hit dozens of small settlements, farms and ranches at the same time. The complaints will come pouring in, as usual, that the army is totally inadequate and inefficient. The devil take 'em! Hell man, we can't be all places at one time!'

'Perhaps you should have remembered that sir when you rode roughshod over Satanta,' Hazen told his superior quietly. 'No chief likes to lose face in front of his warriors. And as for the way they fight, they do what they do best – just as we do. The United States Army has proved itself supreme in set-piece battles so they'd be foolish to even think about fighting us our way. No, they are born guerrillas. They've fought that way with success for centuries. Can't see them abandoning such a tried and trusted formula after all these years. Yes sir, thanks to you, it could well be one hell of a winter.' And he walked off, leaving Sheridan practically foaming at the mouth.

But, as was frequently the case, the generals were wrong yet again. Except that, on this occasion, it was to their advantage. Sensing trickery, in the form of a sneak attack by the army on some, or all, of the five tribes, most of the Kiowas, Comanches and Kiowa-Apaches made straight for the sanctuary of Fort Cobb which they reached in mid-October. Unfortunately for military planning, so did the majority of the Southern Cheyennes and Arapahoes.

So what was Hazen to do when he arrived at Fort Cobb and found them waiting for him? In his mind there were no alternatives; so he fed them and ordered immediate additional supplies of flour, sugar and coffee to augment his rapidly dwindling stocks in order to see his Indian charges through the winter months. He also advised them to remain close to the post – well away from the far-ranging punitive expeditions under the overall leadership of General Sheridan.

But at least two Kiowa chiefs and their followers failed to arrive at Fort Cobb. Satanta and Kicking Bird. Satanta, together with Walks-Like-A-Shadow, Bull Shoulders and several other leading fighters of the Kiowa nation, were on one of their numerous annual forays into Texas to obtain sufficient stocks to see them through the winter. While Kicking Bird, careful not to attack white people but still a Kiowa warrior at heart, had ridden deep into Colorado with his men to plunder the Ute Indians with the same end in mind – the stocking up of winter provisions.

Unfortunately for Satanta, one of Sheridan's punitive columns in the field that winter was under the command of a young glory-seeking, homicidal psychopath named Lieutenant Colonel George Armstrong Custer, of the Seventh Cavalry. Known as the 'Boy General' during the American Civil War, he had been brevetted a major general for his almost suicidal escapades on behalf of the North. Many of his men had died but Custer had survived the war. And, more than anything else, he wanted that brevet rank of general to be made permanent.

# Chapter Five

It was November 26. Custer's troopers were whip-lashed by the driving snow into a state that was neither total pain nor total numbness, as they urged their weary horses through the deep snowdrifts which are such a common feature of the Southern Plains winters. They were also tired almost to the verge of absolute exhaustion and hungry practically to the edge of apparent starvation. Some were frost-bitten. Some were snow blind. Others were simply past caring. But still they kept on. It was madness. Yet even this was preferable, if only slightly so, to the punishments they had seen other men suffer after falling short of the harsh disciplinary standards enforced upon them by the sadistic Custer. If one thing kept them all in motion, it was a common-bond fear of their commander.

Among those capable of thinking with any degree of clarity there seemed to be only one way out of this frozen desolation. Find some damned redskins – it mattered not which tribe – beat them into total submission and then, with an elated Custer eager to report the details of his victory to the eastern newspapermen waiting back at the fort, return to their warm bunks and sleep for as long as they could. Oh, for a fire, some hot grub and a bottle of whisky!

They were moving southward, deeper into Indian

Territory and fording the treacherous icy waters of the South Canadian River, when a courier reached them from the scouting party ahead. There was a trail leading south-east, he told Custer. It had been made by Indians, although he did not know of which tribe or tribes, and it was less than twenty-four hours old. It was the spur that Custer needed. And, when word soon spread back to his men, they suddenly found the going easier – but not much!

Yet they were still too slow for Custer. He was like a kill-crazy dog straining at the leash, turning around every few minutes to snap and snarl at the thing which held him back. The quarry had been scented and he wanted the kill so badly that he could almost taste the blood already. 'You lousy, idle, milk-sucking sons-of-bitches,' he shouted into the wind. 'Get your blue back-sides moving!'

They saw him turn, some even saw his mouth open but no one heard his words. On such occasions bad weather was almost a blessing. 'It's an ill wind . . .' thought one sergeant and found his neck muscles pulled into sudden and vicious pain by the simple act of grinning.

Still they struggled on, through snow more than a foot deep. A few hours before midnight they were ordered to rest for one hour. They sank to the ground, ate bread and drank hot coffee, nodded off for a few minutes of precious sleep only to be prodded awake again almost immediatedly. Then, back into their saddles, backsides no longer quite as cold but now aching with an intense fury, and on the move again. This time there was a ghost-like silence to the column for they had all been ordered to tie down anything that might rattle or make any noise whatever. Nothing but the sounds of hooves crunching in the snow and leather creaking.

To add to the eeriness, the scene was now illuminated by the pale white light of the rising moon. But more ominous still, for the unsuspecting Indians who had made the trail and who had no reason even to attempt to conceal their movements, was the fact that the moonlight showed clearly that the tracks were in the general direction of the Washita River. The river that led to Fort Cobb in the south-east. The river along the banks of which the peaceful members of the five Southern Tribes had been instructed to pitch their tepees that winter so that they would not be mistakenly attacked as hostiles by Sheridan's expedition.

Two Osage Indian scouts, in the pay of the military, reported to Custer about midnight that they could smell woodsmoke ahead. Soon they came upon the glowing remains of a fire. The Osage scouts, with those skills learned only by people of the wilderness, were able to tell with accuracy that the fire had been made by Indian youths looking after a herd of ponies. More important, there was a village close by. Were they sure, growled Custer. They swore that it was so. And they were right. It was the village of the Washita. If Custer knew, or even guessed, the nature of the village, he told no one. He had come hundreds of miles in search of Indians. And Indians he had found. He could almost feel those general's stars upon his shoulders.

Soon one of the Osages, Little Beaver, motioned to Custer to follow him to the crest of a nearby hill. The colonel did so. Yes, he could see where the scout was pointing. Yes, by God, he could discern, if only faintly, the outlines of one group of tepees. Then his excitement grew as his ears detected the various familiar noises of an Indian encampment. The barking dogs, the sounds of a pony herd, the cry of a baby. They were there alright – his Indians and his next rung upward on the ladder of promotion. And he estimated that there were but a few hundred in the camp so he was more than a match for them. Add to this the element of surprise and he could not lose.

Back with his men he divided them into four columns. Quietly they surrounded the village. There were still several hours before the dawn onslaught planned by the former 'Boy General' with his flowing blonde hair, his drooping moustache and his receding chin. The men were bitterly cold but they waited in complete silence and absolute stillness. When their colonel issued an order, it was like receiving a commandment from the Lord. No, upon reflection, it was easier to listen to the word of God. If you acted contrary to his commands it was by no means certain that you would be punished for your disobedience. But the wrath of Custer in such a situation was absolutely certain. And the penalty could mean, and had meant on certain occasions in the past, death by firing squad.

At last the light of the rising sun began to push the semi-darkness away. The shadowy features of the camp and the surrounding landscape developed a clarity of pure crystal as the sun rose triumphantly from behind a distant ridge. The Southern Cheyenne Indians in the tepees below slumbered on.

The troopers advanced slowly upon the cluster of lodges and their unsuspecting inhabitants. But the village dogs were alerted by the unfamiliar sights and sounds around them. They commenced barking. A lone

Indian crawled from his tepee, rifle in hand, to find out what had disturbed them. He saw. And he fired his rifle a fraction of a second later. The shot brought the camp to life – and death!

With trumpeters sounding the charge, Custer's men swarmed in from every side. The Southern Cheyennes trapped in the village were the people of Chief Black Kettle. The same Chief Black Kettle who had seen so many of his followers butchered exactly four years previously during the infamous Sand Creek Massacre when far more women and children than warriors were either shot or cut down by the volunteer cavalry of Colonel John M. Chivington, a Methodist preacher in civilian life. Black Kettle and his wife ran from their lodge. It could not be true! The general at Fort Cobb had given his word. The chief shouted at the soldiers! But they were too busy releasing, in a frenzy of killing, all the tension created by Custer's unrelenting discipline during the long, cold march to the village. Within minutes both Black Kettle and his wife were dead.

Battle-hardened Southern Cheyenne warriors found small pockets of protection behind boulders, in ravines and even in the river where they pressed themselves hard against the banks, up to their armpits in freezing water. They fought a rearguard action so that their comrades would have a better chance of escape.

But it was hopeless. Women and children screamed as bullets tore into their bodies and sabres sliced through their flesh. Some jumped into the river but drowned in the freezing current while trying to swim to safety on the other side.

Before the blood-bath was ended, one hundred and three Indians had been killed, including many women and children, in a massacre which was no less savage and no more justifiable than the one at Sand Creek on November 29, 1864. A total of fifty-three women and children were herded into captivity. A thousand buffalo robes, immense stores of food, blankets, clothing, all the tepees and everything they contained which was of no use to the souvenir-hungry troopers were destroyed upon Custer's commands. He also ordered the cold-blooded slaughter of eight hundred Indian ponies captured during the attack on the village.

As soon as the orgy of destruction was complete, Custer vacated the area at the double. He had been told by a captive squaw that the village was only a small part of a vast Indian encampment stretching for many miles along the river. There were literally thousands of Kiowas, Comanches, Kiowa-Apaches and Araphoes spending the winter camped alongside the Washita at the invitation of the blue-coat general at Fort Cobb, the woman prisoner told him. The colonel led his men due north to Camp Supply, the nearest army post with any guarantee of safety.

In his indecent haste to escape the possible vengeance of these other warriors, Custer committed the army's cardinal sin. He left behind a brother officer and his detachment of sixteen men. They were all killed in the fight with the Southern Cheyennes. The officer was Major Joel Elliott of the Medicine Lodge peace talks. The army accepted Custer's invented explanation of the Washita massacre when he blatantly told his superiors that he had followed a band of active hostiles into Black Kettle's village. But it never quite forgave him for deserting Major Elliott and his men.

On the morning of December 17 Custer was returning

to Fort Cobb with his men when one of his scouts drew his attention to a group of horsemen riding towards them from the distant horizon. As the riders drew nearer the colonel became somewhat apprehensive. It was a large war-party of several hundred Kiowa warriors under the leadership of Satanta and Lone Wolf. The Indians were in full war paint.

Satanta signalled that he wanted to parley under a white flag of truce; so Custer rode forward accompanied by several officers and about fifty scouts. With a wide grin Satanta moved in closer but with much fewer men. Round one to the chief. He had less men to guard him than did Custer. Hence, according to Indian logic, he was not as afraid of the colonel as the colonel was afraid of him.

Both leaders had interpreters. Satanta ignored Custer's man and conducted the meeting through Walks-Like-A-Shadow. Round two to the Kiowa chief. The colonel was an easy man to arouse and rapidly became irritated by the ploys of Satanta.

'You tell your chiefs that I'm not here to play games!' Custer almost shouted at Walks-Like-A-Shadow. 'You tell him to listen damn carefully to what I have to say.'

The Kiowa chief grinned at his fellow war Leader, Lone Wolf. 'He sounds like a man who has just found a scorpion in his trousers,' commented Satanta. 'Angry and a little frightened. But not sure what he should do to stop himself from being stung by it.' Lone Wolf started to laugh.

'What's so goddam funny?' demanded Custer. 'What in the hell have they got to laugh about?'

'Small thing. Not important,' replied the young Kiowa interpreter, struggling with great difficulty to suppress his own amusement at Satanta's comments. 'I tell them what you say about listen careful to you.'

As he translated the colonel's words into the Kiowa tongue, both Satanta and Lone Wolf stopped grinning. 'You tell him that we will listen to what he has to say,' answered Satanta. 'But you will tell him also to use his eyes as well as his mouth. Tell him to look around at my many fighting men before making any threats he cannot keep.'

After a while Custer calmed down sufficiently to agree that the Kiowas be allowed to ride on to Fort Cobb and to camp there under the protection promised them by General Hazen. Then, fuming at his own impotence and loss of face in front of a band of what he contemptuously referred to as 'lousy red savages', he jerked his horse's head around viciously and stormed off, followed by his scouts and their officers. As he rode back to his waiting column, an almost uncontrollable rage ate into his mind like an incurable cancer. 'I'll bring these red bastards to their knees if it's the last thing I do,' he muttered from between teeth clenched so tightly that blood oozed from a small puncture in his lower lip.

As Custer's column restarted its interrupted march, it was joined by Satanta, Lone Wolf, Walks-Like-A-Shadow, Bull Shoulders and other warriors who had offered to accompany the soldiers as an indication of their good faith. Through Walks-Like-A-Shadow, Satanta had explained to Custer that the rest of his people would follow at a slower pace as their ponies were mainly in a sorry state due to the usual lack of forage that forever weakened their mounts throughout the winter months.

That Custer had a truly vicious temper, few people denied. That he was impetuous and daring, often beyond the border line of common sense and well into the realm of recklessness, was equally undeniable. But that he was also stupid was an accusation that could not be levelled at him as an acceptable truth by even his most ardent enemies – and he had made enough of these during his brief career already to suffice most men for their entire lives.

But the Indians chose to equate the colonel's earlier behaviour with that of a simpleton. Yet they were fooling only themselves as, a few at a time, they dropped out of the line of march with the explanation that they had to leave in order to help their exhausted families reach the sanctuary of Fort Cobb. Custer was taken in not at all. He simply waited until Satanta and Lone Wolf were the sole Kiowas riding with the column, knowing that their code of honour would prevent them leaving until the rest of their warriors had departed, and then he arrested them. Both men were placed under close guard. It was December 18. They reached Fort Cobb two days later.

Waiting for them at the post was General Sheridan. With his winter campaign rapidly developing into a military farce and appearing to go every way other than the way he had planned, the general was in a tempestuous mood. He had expected all the Kiowas to arrive at Fort Cobb but all he had was Satanta and Lone Wolf.

Sheridan waited for two days. Then he had both war chiefs brought to his office. 'You have exactly forty-eight hours, two whole days, to get your tribe to come into this fort,' he told them in a tone colder than the ice outside. 'If your people are not here in this time then you will both hang. And that, my red-skinned friends, is a genuine twenty-four-carat-gold Sheridan promise. Believe me.'

61

Both Satanta and Lone Wolf pleaded with the general for more time in which to gather their tribe together. 'They are scattered throughout many parts,' protested Lone Wolf. 'We can never reach them in so short a time. It is hopeless to even attempt such a thing.'

'Well, you'd better try gentlemen; for two days is all the time you have,' repeated Sheridan and they suddenly knew, with a gut-twisting certainty, that he meant precisely what he said.

'Can we send runners out?' asked Satanta who had seen both Walks-Like-A-Shadow and his close friend Bull Shoulders just before he had ridden into the fort with Custer's command.

'Yes, that much I will allow,' agreed the general.

The two young warriors were sent for. 'We will do everything in our power,' Walks-Like-A-Shadow assured Satanta after the Kiowa chief had explained tersely the situation in which he and Lone Wolf now found themselves.

Within hours the two friends had rounded up several other warriors. Riding in pairs, each couple headed for all the places in which their people might be encamped. Almost asleep on their hard driven ponies, aching with pain, freezing and hungry, the riders achieved what had appeared an absolute impossibility when they set out. Riding through the night as well as during daylight, they began to stumble across one camp after another. By the afternoon of the second day groups of Kiowas began to trickle into Fort Cobb to stop the two leaders from being executed. And by that nightfall the tribe, apart from a few individuals and small bands way out on the Staked Plains, had reached the post. Satanta and Lone Wolf had been saved from hanging. How many white nations would have done likewise to gain the reprieve of but two leaders and at considerable risk to their own lives?

The end of December saw nearly every member of both the Kiowa and Comanche tribes encamped within the environs of Fort Cobb. However, they did not have the appearance of people who had been defeated. Looking out from a mess window one day with his field binoculars, Sheridan watched the Indians closely for an hour or so as they moved around the fort intent on their various tasks.

After a while he turned to a junior officer and remarked: 'Look at them. Do they look beaten to you? I don't think that they even consider themselves our prisoners. I mean, do they look a defeated bunch to you?'

'No sir,' replied the junior officer, a young lieutenant. 'I haven't seen too many people in a situation of submission as yet, as I haven't been out here very long. But they certainly don't behave as I would expect fighting men in their position to behave.'

'Precisely,' agreed Sheridan. 'You've hit the nail bang on the head. They simply don't realise that they're a conquered race. They haven't even begun to accept defeat. I'll wager that they're just waiting until Satanta and Lone Wolf are set free and then they'll be off again. Up to their old tricks. Hit and run raids all over the countryside. From south into Mexico and up to the Canadian border in the north if they've a mind to. Then Washington will be after my guts for garters again. Well son, what would you do in my place, eh?'

'Well sir, I know it has a treacherous sound to it,' answered the lieutenant, 'But I'd hang on to the one thing that keeps them as they are now.'

'Satanta and Lone Wolf you mean?'

'Yes sir. I know it's not playing by the rules but I honestly don't know what else I could do.'

'By God boy, you're right. Keep the two of 'em locked up and the rest will stay on their best behaviour for fear I might hang 'em both.'

So neither Satanta nor Lone Wolf were set free despite frequent protests from their people. At best it was an uneasy truce but it did give Sheridan a tenuous hold over both the Kiowas and their allies, the Comanches, until the general could find a site further south than Fort Cobb which would be better located to protect the frontier of Texas from possible future Indian incursions.

Colonel Benjamin H. Grierson, commanding officer of the Tenth Cavalry, the first negro regiment to be established by the U.S. Army, was also in command of the District of the Indian Territory. He had led his coloured troopers, called buffalo soldiers by the Indians because of the similarity of their tightly curled black hair to that found on the shoulders of the American bison, over thousands of miles of the area in attempts to subdue the Southern Plains tribes. And he felt he had the answer to his general's problems. About thirty-five miles south of Fort Cobb, at the place where Medicine Bluff and Cache Creek met one another, there was a region with plentiful supplies of grass, water and building materials.

A team of officers inspected the area and agreed that it was ideally situated for the proposed new post. Despite freezing weather, winter storms and flooded streams, Sheridan immmediatedly evacuated Fort Cobb and marched to the new site where building began on January 10, 1869. The new post was named Fort Sill.

As the fort's structures rapidly began to take shape – sub-zero temperatures proving a superb incentive for the swift erection of buildings to protect their constructors from the unpredictable ravages of a typical plains' winter – so Sheridan's attitude towards the Kiowas and Comanches began to soften somewhat. Throughout the rest of January and into February he held a series of councils with the chiefs of the two tribes. He lectured them severely concerning their actions following the Medicine Lodge Treaty and threatened that any similar violations in the future would invite immediate and violent retribution. But if they continued along their present path of peace then all would go well between them and their white overlords. To show his good will towards them all he set free both Satanta and Lone Wolf.

# Chapter Six

Spring at Fort Sill that year brought with it a beauty such as only the Southern Plains can stage. The streams gurgled, bubbled, plopped, hissed and babbled with excitement at the start of their incredibly long and eventful journey to the distant Gulf of Mexico. Their flowing waters sparkled with a myriad white flashes, like so many flawless diamonds, as the rays of the sun danced upon their rippling surfaces. The clarity of the streams also readily revealed to the spirited Indian children who played along their banks, worlds of wonder beneath those same twinkling surfaces. With the dead of winter behind them and the strength of summer yet to come, it was a time for happiness and laughter. And Indian children were no different from other children of freedom the world over.

The cottonwood trees were newly clad in green. The grass was shedding its yellow and brown blades of winter and displaying its many hues of rich green that came with its annual rebirth. Amidst its roots could be seen the shoots of countless wild flowers that would soon turn the meadows into carpets of scarlet, yellow, purple, orange and green. The shrill chirping of the transparent-winged cicadas could be heard from among the leaves of the trees. As well as the ever-present cottonwoods, there were also shady groves of elms and pecans. All these trees were now the homes of many birds of varied plumage and equally diverse voices.

Everywhere the plains were vibrant with countless forms of wild life. From the millions of darting insects that inhabited the earth beneath its grassroots to the ponderous herds of bison that rumbled above, crushing those same roots with their splayed hooves as they grazed upon the grass itself. To the numerous Indians of the plains, whether Nez Perces, Crows and Blackfeet of the northern grasslands, Sioux and Cheyennes of the central prairies or Kiowas and Comanches of the Southern Plains, these massive beasts were the source of all things necessary for these people to retain their nomadic ways of life.

The bison, more popularly known to Americans as the buffalo, was a commissary on four legs to all plains Indians. It supplied them with meat – no edible part ever being left unconsumed, clothing, homes, blankets, tools, weapons, cordage, glue, cosmetics, drink in the form of blood whenever the situation demanded it and fuel. In the vast treeless areas of the prairies the dried deposits of dung called buffalo chips, were the only available fuel for cooking fires and as a source of heat during cold spells. Without the buffalo the tribes of the American grasslands knew that their culture would be doomed.

Although clumsy in appearance and extremely nearsighted, the buffalo has a keen sense of smell and can move at great speed whenever spurred into activity. To the earliest American plains Indians this often meant long periods of hunger. For, on foot, and with only primitive stone weapons, they were seldom able to bring down these gigantic creatures. The only method that brought them any kind of success was to surround a small herd and scare it into stampeding to death over a nearby cliff. However, this was extremely wasteful as they always killed far more than they needed.

Then the Spaniards brought horses into North America from Mexico as they rode them northward during numerous attempts to subdue these nomadic people. They were unsuccessful. The land, the climate and the warrior nomads themselves combined to beat the un-invited Spanish visitors. But, inevitably, some of their mounts ran off. Left wild and free to roam the prairies they soon bred prolifically. It was not long before the Indians learned to capture and ride these strange animals.

Almost overnight their world changed. They now had horses. They could travel as far and as fast as the buffalo upon which their lives depended. It was now possible to trade – or raid – into distant places. They could carry so much more wherever they chose to go with such great beasts of burden. No longer were they dependent upon their own backs or those of their dogs for transporting goods. No more chasing herds of buffalo over precipices in order to kill them. Selected animals could be brought down individually by galloping on horseback alongside the chosen beast and killing it with lance or bow and arrow. The plains Indians had reached their peak with the culture of the horse.

For the Kiowas at Fort Sill the spring of 1869 was no different from all those that had preceded it. Gone was winter, called by them 'The time our babies cry for food.' Now was the time for hunting the buffalo for fresh meat with which to fill their shrunken stomachs. Government rations had sustained them through the cold months but they had been sparse and of inferior quality as a result of rampant corruption among American officials.

One morning Walks-Like-A-Shadow asked his friend Bull Shoulders if he would join him and several other braves for the first buffalo hunt of the year. Bull Shoulders agreed and within the time it took to round up a band of equally eager hunters, gather their weapons and saddle their mounts, the chase was under way.

It was a perfect day for the hunt. The sky was an unblemished blue save for the white hot disc which was the sun. Yet it was not the heat of summer and a pleasantly cool wind blew ceaselessly among them carrying with it the perfume of countless wild flowers. Robins, cardinals and woodthrush could be heard in the trees behind them as they rode away from Fort Sill.

As the party moved out across the lush grasslands its members caught occasional glimpses of various species of deer. They saw a large band of antelope. The warm spring weather had also brought out several bears along the bottoms and numerous types of lesser game and birds among the higher reaches of nearby canyons. It was a paradise for hunters. Normally the Kiowas would have been happy to take home deer, antelope or other game. But they would let nothing entice them from their chosen path on this hallowed occasion. There was nothing quite like the first buffalo hunt of any spring.

But during recent years, mused Walks-Like-A-Shadow as they rode, it seemed to take longer each spring to find the buffalo; and the apparently endless herds that had covered the plains in his childhood now looked considerably smaller. There had been a time when he had told himself that this was simply a result of growing up. A childs's imagination tended to exaggerate virtually everything with which he came into contact. Big was gigantic. And hundreds became thousands. But he was no longer convinced that the apparent diminution in the vast herds of buffalo was the result of an end to child-hood illusions. Somehow, for some reason, the herds really were decreasing in size and numbers, he told himself.

He watched as Bull Shoulders and two other braves broke away from the main group and galloped rapidly ahead, yelling loudly and excitedly as they spurred their mounts with that almost uncontrollable exuberance that marked the end of winter's lethargy; fanning out in three separate directions – left, centre and right – scouting for buffalo. Deep in thought, he almost forgot to acknowl-edge Bull Shoulder's wave as his friend charged past him.

That they would find buffalo, Walks-Like-A-Shadow had no doubt. But these huge lumbering beasts, without which the tribes could not exist, would have wandered even deeper into the southern grasslands than the pre-vious year and they would be found in much smaller bands than before. These things he knew, without having to wait for the return of Bull Shoulders and the other two.

The white men killed buffalo for food as they crossed the prairies. There were cavalry troopers policing the plains, miners still heading for all points west seeking those elusive pots of gold at each rainbow's end and wagon trains of settlers steadily winding their ways to the rich agricultural lands of California and Oregon. But there were more than sufficient buffalo and other game for their needs and to meet the requirements of the plains Indians – the healthy annual reproductive cycles of the teeming wildlife of the lush prairie lands ensured this.

Or should have. Walks-Like-A-Shadow was puzzled. Something was happening to the buffalo. But what?

There was an atmosphere of despondency among the members of the hunting party as they sat around their fires that evening. It was the only occasion any of them could recall when the first day of a spring hunt had ended without the sighting of even a solitary buffalo. Not that they were hungry. In fact they had eaten well. For Bull Shoulders and the other pair had killed two large deer after meeting together on their way back to the pre-arranged night camp.

Each of the three scouts told the same story. A day of non-stop riding without fresh signs of buffalo in any direction. Tracks that were not new had been plentiful. Many piles of dung which, when broken open, were dry right through. A clear indication that the buffalo had passed that way many days previously. There was not the usual happy camp fire banter that first evening. No telling of tall stories. All of them fell asleep early or pretended to. It was going to be a long hunt. And there would be many anxious Kiowas awaiting their return to Fort Sill with their pack horses laden with buffalo meat and skins.

The sun had barely peered above the crests of the distant grey-blue, haze enshrouded hills before the Kiowas were once more on horseback, diligently following the stale tracks of the herds which appeared to lead them ever southward. Few words were spoken. There was not the laughter of yesterday. Just thoughts of today, tomorrow and the following days that it would take before they found their quarry.

The second day ended as dismally as the first. The third was no different from the second. But on the fourth day a warrior came riding in excitedly from way out on their left flank. 'Over there! Over there!' he shouted, pointing back along the way he had come, as he reined his lathered, foamed-flecked pony alongside those of Walks-Like-A-Shadow and Bull Shoulders.

'What is it?' demanded Bull Shoulders. 'Fresh sign? How new are the tracks?'

'I am not talking of buffalo tracks,' replied the rider, a young warrior who, for reasons which were self-evident, was labelled for life with the unflattering name of Short Legs. 'I am talking of buffalo. Many of them.'

'Then you must have the eyes of a hawk in flight,' retorted Bull Shoulders, 'For I can see no buffalo.'

'That is because they are concealed by the long grass,' Short Legs replied impatiently. 'They are . . .'

'Then they must be extremely small buffalo,' interrupted Bull Shoulders with a cynical snort. 'Or you must have an extremely large imagination!'

'You may have a big body Bull Shoulders but your brain must indeed be very little. Allow me to finish what I was saying and then you will see . . .'

Bull Shoulders edged his mount close to Short Legs' pony and raised his right arm. His huge fist resembled a massive knot of wood at the end of an equally stout cudgel.

Before he could bring his fist down upon its obvious target, the head of the young warrior who seemed to enjoy the hazards involved in taunting the much bigger man, Walks-Like-A-Shadow drove his horse roughly between their two mounts and forced them apart. 'Stop this stupidity – both of you!' he ordered, his voice ominously low. 'Now Short Legs, finish what you were telling us.'

'I was about to say that it is impossible to see the buffalo from here because they are all dead.'

'Dead?' echoed Walks-Like-A-Shadow along with several others.

'Yes,' answered Short Legs. 'With nothing but their skins taken from them. And the rest of their bodies just great piles of meat left rotting in the sun. Their carcases are swarming with maggots.'

'But this is a thing without sense,' remarked Bull Shoulders, his quick temper having subsided equally as rapidly as it had flared up. 'Who would do this thing and why?'

'Let us ride over and see if we can uncover the reasons for such a terrible waste of meat,' commented Walks-Like-A-Shadow as he kneed his horse round and jogged it steadily through the tall coarse grass, permitting Short Legs to overtake him and lead them to the buffalo carcases. As they drew near, the stench of the decaying flesh reached their nostrils several seconds before their eyes saw the dead animals. It was exactly as Short Legs had said. Literally hundreds of buffalo corpses, bloated, mutilated and crawling with countless maggots; all their hides ripped off and carted away.

They had obviously been dead for some days because many of them showed clearly the savage, slashing, tearing talon, beak, claw and teeth marks, no longer fresh, left by the buzzards, coyotes and other scavengers of the plains.

'Something must have scared them off completely,' remarked Bull Shoulders, 'Otherwise they would have returned to finish off all this meat. No buzzard or coyote would willingly have left unfinished such a feast as this.'

'Not unless there were even fresher carcases to be found not too far off,' commented Short Legs, his eyes staring into the hazy distance.

'What makes you say this?' queried Walks-Like-A-Shadow.

'Because these dead buffalo are stretched in a line which points but one way,' replied Short Legs. 'The grass around here is trampled down over a considerable area and has been grazed upon by the buffalo in many places. It seems to me that someone, several people in fact, started killing them at this spot and that they began milling around in panic at first. Then they stampeded in the direction marked clearly by the line of dead animals. The channel of grass trampled by their hooves is much narrower and has been churned up by buffalo in flight and not by peacefully grazing herds.

'Whoever did this killing planned well,' he continued, 'For it is obvious to me that they intended the herds to stampede in the direction that they did.'

'How do you know all these things?' scoffed the quick-tempered Bull Shoulders who, even his friend Walks-Like-A-Shadow noticed, was becoming meaner of late, easier to arouse and ever-ready to carry grudges he would once have forgotten in but a short time.

'Because I have never let the white man's whisky dull my senses!' retorted Short Legs. 'You have developed such a taste and thirst for this fiery poison that you no longer see things as a Kiowa warrior should.'

Hatred blazed in the big man's eyes. 'One day little man you will regret having said these things. I will have you crying out for mercy when this hunt is over.'

'I think not,' replied Short Legs calmly, 'Because not only do you think slower these days but you react much slower also. Whereas I am just as good with my weapons as I ever was.'

There was an ominous silence as the two men faced one another. Walks-Like-A-Shadow watched them and suddenly felt tired. He had suspected it but had pretended not to see what he had no desire to see. His friend from childhood, Bull Shoulders, had become addicted to the white man's drink, which put fire in a man's belly but while so doing took the strength from his brain and also from all other parts of his body. This was a sad time for, until recently, the two of them had spent much of their lives together and shared many experiences. But Walks-Like-A-Shadow knew he could no longer pretend not to see his friend's new weakness.

He spoke to Bull Shoulders. 'You will forget this thing between the two of you,' he told him. 'Short Legs is not your enemy. If you wish to bear malice within you, then carry it for those Americans who sell you their crazy drink so readily. There will be no more talk of fighting among brother Kiowas. Is that clear enough to both of you?'

Bull Shoulders and Short Legs nodded and turned away from one another. Neither man spoke. The silence, brief though it was, was broken by Walks-Like-A-Shadow.

'Tell us Short Legs why you feel so certain about the buffalo stampede,' he said.

'Because whoever started it, wanted it so,' answered Short Legs. 'If not, why did they station marksmen along the line of flight to shoot down the buffalo even as they fled. See how well the carcases are spaced out. No, they knew which way the buffalo would run because they made them take that way. There are no pony tracks alongside those of the fleeing buffalo so this was no mass killing from on horseback.

'And I found large balls of lead in several of the carcases which showed that they entered the bodies low down and travelled upwards. This is how it would be if the buffalo were shot by men lying down waiting for them. And the accuracy of the shooting meant that they had much time in which to aim. When we shoot buffalo by riding beside them on our ponies, then our bullets go downwards through their bodies. And, because we are moving as we shoot, it sometimes takes many bullets to kill one animal. But each buffalo I saw today had been shot only once. Good shots too. And all the lead balls come from the big rifles which white hunters use. Not from ordinary rifles like we and American soldiers fire in battle. All these things I know. But why they take away only skins and not meat I do not understand. It is most strange and also most wasteful.'

'It is indeed strange and wasteful,' agreed Walks-Like-A-Shadow. 'And, because it is so, it is a bad thing for the Kiowas. We need the buffalo to live. But the men responsible for this slaughter are chasing them further away each year from our hunting grounds and also making the numbers of buffalo much smaller. This type of killing is not good. If we do not stop it from happening then, in years to come, there will be no more buffalo for the Kiowas. Then who knows what will happen to our tribe which is already steadily decreasing in size all the time?'

Short Legs spoke. 'I think that while most of us search for buffalo to take back to our people, some of us should follow this trail of death to discover why it is so.'

A chorus of agreement from the Kiowa hunters greeted

his suggestion. One of the warriors, called Eight Toes as a result of a shooting accident when playing with his father's loaded gun while still a toddler, rode up to Walks-Like-A-Shadow. 'Why don't you take two others with you, perhaps Short Legs and Bull Shoulders, and follow this trail while the rest of us hunt buffalo,' he suggested. 'Then, later at the village, when we meet together again, you can tell us whatever you find out and then the chiefs will decide what to do to stop this terrible slaughter of our buffalo.'

'Why take Short Legs?' grumbled Bull Shoulders like a petulant child.

'Because today he has shown all of us here what a great tracker he is,' countered Eight Toes.

'Pah, it is only because his eyes are so much closer to the ground than ours are that he sees things which we do not,' grunted Bull Shoulders.

'Whatever the reason,' interceded Walks-Like-A-Shadow, anxious to avoid further argument and eager not to waste any more time, 'He has done that which I had previously considered impossible. I have a reputation for being an excellent tracker but today Short Legs proved that he can walk softer than a shadow.'

There was an outburst of spontaneous laughter for the Kiowas, hardened fighters that they were, enjoyed a joke just as do bands of seasoned warriors anywhere in the world. The tension was broken. Walks-like-A-Shadow felt a great relief. He slowly expelled the breath he had been holding, felt the muscles of his body go pleasantly slack and his previously taut frame readjust itself to a position in the saddle of far greater comfort.

Eager to maintain this welcome atmosphere of relaxation he spoke again, once more choosing his words with the wisdom of a tribal diplomat. 'Eight Toes has made a good suggestion. But I feel that it should be for Bull Shoulders, who has so often proved himself a great hunter, to lead the search for live buffalo. Our people are hungry for fresh meat and I know Bull Shoulders is one person who is capable of bringing back a quick kill. Whereas I, together with Short Legs and Mountain Cat, will follow the dead buffalo trail.'

The reference to the twin trails of live buffalo and dead buffalo brought forth another bout of easy laughter. They were all relaxed once again and this was good for everyone concerned. But, more important, he had arranged it so that Bull Shoulders and Short Legs rode in separate groups while retaining the much needed tracking skills of the latter for his own use and, at the same time, restoring some of the former's earlier prestige.

Even Satank or Satanta could not have done better in such a situation, he mused as the two groups parted – each band wishing the other good hunting as they rode their chosen ways.

# Chapter Seven

The mood of Walks-Like-A-Shadow, Short Legs and Mountain Cat, also selected because of his trailing abilities, was like that of one person as they followed the blood-soaked, stench-filled path of wanton slaughter. Each man was grim, determined and greatly puzzled.

They rode for mile after mile. The ugliness of the countless buffalo carcases they passed made them totally oblivious to the beauty around them. A beauty in which they would normally have revelled had the circumstances been other than they were.

Occasionally they came across small areas of flattened grass, dotted with empty cartridge cases, that showed where men had remained patiently prone to shoot down the terror-stricken beasts and to ensure that they kept to the route their ruthless killers had selected. At other times they saw distant specks in the cloudless azure sky. Specks that betrayed themselves into easy recognition by the way they soared and swooped in circles. Buzzards. More dead buffalo.

Once or twice one or other of the three relentless trackers thought he heard gunshots. But not one of them was capable in his particular state of mind to separate the sounds of reality from those of his desires. So each stayed silent. And, by so doing, knew not whether the others did or did not hear the rifle shots he sometimes thought his ears detected. The possibility of ridicule can often turn out to be an unnecessarily burdensome riding companion to any man engaged in so vital a hunt.

So absorbed in their sole objective were the three Kiowas that not one of them made any reference to those necessities of life which sustain all people everywhere no matter what they are doing. Thus, there was no stopping for food, water or rest. Nor even to shade themselves from the remorseless sun which pounded its searing heat into their perspiring, glistening red-brown bodies – like a white hot hammer beating against so many pieces of shining copper in order to mould them into metallic robots with but one automatic, monotonous forward motion. But these were not robots in human form. They were humans. And human bodies can endure but a certain amount of pressure before breaking down.

That breaking point for one of them, Mountain Cat, came on the afternoon of the second day. He ignored the light-headed sensation which caused him to see and hear things which did not exist beyond the bounds of his distorted senses. But he could not ignore the sudden blackness which seized his tortured brain and pitched him from his horse's back like a child's discarded rag doll.

Short Legs saw Mountain Cat fall to the ground. But, after so many hours of mechanical movement in the saddle, it took several seconds for the significance of what he had seen to cause any reaction in his dulled mind. He slowly reined his pony to a halt and shouted at Walks-Like-A-Shadow who had been riding in the lead for some time now. But the shout was not a shout.

Instead it was but a feeble croak. Short Legs' lips were dry and split. His throat felt as if hundreds of tiny daggers were stabbing his voice to death.

The pain brought an agonising grimace to his face. Pain. Here, at least, was something that brought a positive reaction from the little man. He picked up a pebble and hurled it, with all the strength he could muster, in the direction of Walks-Like-A-Shadow. He was lucky. It struck him in the middle of his back.

Walks-Like-A-Shadow turned round slowly, pulling his mount to a standstill as he did so. Through the haziness which had been his sole riding companion for what seemed so long a period that he could barely recall that it had even had a beginning, he saw his two friends not as people but as characters within a dream from which he was trying to wake. Gradually he became aware that he was not asleep and what he saw was real. He turned his horse around and headed towards Short Legs and Mountain Cat who was now in a seated position; forced there by the wiry strength of the smaller man.

Walks-Like-A-Shadow dismounted carefully. He took hold of one of Mountain Cat's arms while Short Legs grasped the other firmly. Slowly they raised the semiconscious warrior to his feet and began to walk him around.

At first he was a dead weight but, as the exercise began to quicken his circulation, so Mountain Cat started to breath deeper and easier. And within several minutes he was standing up unassisted, albeit in a most unsteady manner. He looked totally dejected. It was obvious to the others that he felt ashamed for what had taken place earlier but that he had not the strength to apologise for his apparent failure. Which was just as well, for they were both too weak to have even attempted to dissuade him from reaching such a conclusion.

A quick look over their ponies revealed that they were in little better shape than their riders. Water had to be found – and quickly. So one obsession gave way to another. The hunt for the killers of the buffalo became insignificant compared with the life or death search for water.

The three Kiowas led their horses, not only to conserve the energy of their mounts, without which they would be virtually helpless so far out on the unprotected baking plains of that vast expanse of land known only to the whites as Indian Territory, but also to put life back into their own cramped limbs.

It was almost nightfall before the late evening chorus of birds, obviously not suffering from dry throats, led them to a small, virtually hidden water seep.

Each man drank a little of the life-giving liquid, careful not to disturb the muddy bottom of the tank so as to keep the water as clear and palatable as possible for his comrades. And two would hold back the ponies while the other drank. It was a long time before they had taken in all that they could hold. Then they filled their water bottles.

Finally their horses were allowed to drink; one at a time so that the seep emptied no faster than it filled and also in order to keep the three animals from fighting each other to get at what must have looked to them such a minute puddle of water. The ponies drank last for the simple reason that they never failed, in their eagerness to get at the water, to muddy any waterhole they used. For the mounts it was a time for relaxing in more ways than one. And any man who has been sufficiently foolish, as a result of well-intentioned kindness to his horse, to permit it the luxury of drinking first from any of the West's countless smaller pools, will tell you that a mixture of muddy water and horse urine is a most unpleasant cocktail.

Once the ponies had finished drinking they were ground-reined to nearby bushes so that they could graze at the least sun-dried of the grasses around them. These were the grasses which had been partially protected from the merciless rays of the abnormally hot spring sun by the shrubs clustered above their yellow-green blades.

While the horses munched contentedly, Walks-Like-A-Shadow ghosted his way silently to the bushes and small trees furthest away from the water seep. When he returned he had three dead game birds in his hands. Asleep on the lower branches, they had been killed without even waking. The birds around the three unfortunates heard nothing and slept blissfully on, unaware of how lucky they were while former comrades now cooked steadily over a fire less than a hundred yards away.

That night there was no riding for the Kiowas. They slept until sunrise, their stomachs pleasantly full for the first time in several days and their bodies held clear of the night's frosty fingers by the warmth that emanated from the resolute glow of the fire around which they lay. Experienced dwellers of the plains, they knew exactly how to construct a fire of dry timber interlaced with green wood so as to make it burn steadily for the precise time required.

Morning dawned clear and crisp. A sparkling hoar frost reflected the rays of the rising sun. The earth's cloak of white crystal combined with the flawless blue blanket which was the sky above, to present the three waking

Kiowas with a beauty that even their stiff and aching bodies could not prevent them appreciating.

The night's sleep following the filling of their stomachs, together with the almost unbelievable recuperative powers of their own bodies, had worked wonders. There was not even the slightest doubt concerning what should be done. They spoke cheerfully as they consumed a quick breakfast and prepared their mounts to continue following the tracks that had led them thus far. But their talk was not of whether they should or should not continue their journey along the trail of buffalo carcasses. Instead they jested and poked fun at one another with that same good natured humour found among comrades in arms the world over. The tribulations of yesterday were no longer of any import to their minds. Today was definitely a day for the hunt. And so the hunt continued.

As the sun's rays quickly assumed their full power so the earth's white mantle melted rapidly away. Everywhere, in its place, could be seen the countless hues of the plains in bloom. It was a scene of unmatched beauty and gladdened even the resilient hearts of these three seasoned warriors.

But only for a while. For that same increasing power of the sun which eased the tensions from their aching bodies, also brought with it the return of the rancid stench of the bloated and mutilated corpses which guided them to who knew what or where. By noon the stink was so unbearable that the three pursuers of the buffalo killers slowly and unconsciously widened the gap between themselves and the carcasses.

As a result they were unaware that by the afternoon of this, their third day on the trail, the smell was no longer so powerful. It was Mountain Cat who first noticed that the corpses had a fresher look to them and that birds of carrion were still feasting upon some of them. He called to his two fellow riders.

'See, my dreaming friends,' he said triumphantly, pointing at the dead buffalo. 'The meat is new. These animals have been shot quite recently. Their killers cannot be too far ahead.'

The three men rode closer to the line of carcases. The fresh appearance of the flesh and dried blood lifted their flagging spirits. 'It is clear that we are less than one full day behind those we seek,' commented Walks-Like-A-Shadow. 'It is time for us to move faster. But also with caution. These white butchers may well have scouts out on all sides. Not only to look for buffalo but also to see that no angry Indians catch them unprepared for battle.'

'Why should they think that they might be followed by Indians?' queried Short Legs. 'These are white men with but the minds of white men. Not the minds of Indians.'

'No, these are not just white men,' countered Walks-Like-A-Shadow. 'They are something more. They are experienced hunters. Look how they found the buffalo so quickly. They found them before we did. See how expertly they drove them in the direction they wanted them to go. How cunningly they waited in concealment. And how accurately they shot them down. No, such men should never be under-estimated. I will wager that they have scouts out. And I will wager also that the men who kill our buffalo are also hard fighters. For men with faint hearts would not venture so far into Kiowa and Comanche country. Come, let us ride – but with great care.'

The morning of the fourth day rewarded the relentless purpose of the trio of copper-tinted warriors. The weather was as clear as that of the preceding days so they all heard the unmistakable noise of gunfire coming from somewhere ahead of them. The shots were so many and so rapid that it sounded as if a full-scale battle was in progress.

'It would appear that other warriors have found our quarry already,' commented Mountain Cat, his eyes glowing in eager anticipation at the possibility of a fight. 'Let us ride fast and support our brothers.' He dug his heels hard into the flanks of his pony to increase its speed from the steady pace they had been maintaining throughout their remorseless manhunt.

Walks-Like-A-Shadow galloped after him, then alongside him, then across his front, causing Mountain Cat's pony to swerve from its course to avoid a collision. The eager young Kiowa reined his mount to a standstill. He looked puzzled. 'Why do you stop me?' he asked Walks-Like-A-Shadow. 'Are we not going to help our fellow warriors?'

'I do not think that it is a fight that we hear,' Walks-like-A-Shadow told Mountain Cat and also Short Legs who had now caught up with them.

'Then why is there so much firing?' asked Short Legs. 'Like Mountain Cat I think there is a battle taking place out there between the white men we follow and our Indian brethren.'

Walks-Like-A-Shadow shook his head. 'Listen with greater care,' he said. 'Those are not the sounds of rifles such as we use. They are the sounds of much bigger weapons.'

'Such as the long rifles that white men use for hunting,' interrupted Short Legs.

This time Walks-Like-A-Shadow nodded in agreement.

'But why so much shooting?' interjected Mountain Cat, the look of bewilderment upon his face increasing by the second.

'There can be but one answer to your question,' replied Walks-Like-A-Shadow. 'And that is that the Americans are facing a large herd or several smaller ones.'

Short Legs, his face registering total confusion, looked across at Walks-Like-A-Shadow. 'I feel deep inside me that you are right. But every time I ask myself why should they do this thing I cannot find an answer. If they wished to kill all the buffalo so that our people would be starved into submission then why do they also take the hides from every animal? Such actions must slow down the killing. It makes no sense.'

'Perhaps they have found some use for the hides,' said Walks-Like-a-Shadow. 'But it is not soldiers who do this thing.'

'How do you know?' queried Mountain Cat.

'There are many reasons,' came back the other's reply. 'The rifles they use are not soldier's weapons. Their tracks show that they do not wear army boots. In the places where their sharpshooters lie in ambush for the buffalo I have found buttons and other things which are not the same as those of the pony soldiers. And, when I open the pieces of dung left by their horses, there are no traces of the grain used by the soldiers to feed their ponies. Grass and some grain. But not army grain. There is a difference. To earn his name Walks-Like-A-Shadow learned such things, and many others, a long time ago. Even from when I was a child.'

'But if they are taking the hides with them as they go,' persisted Mountain Cat, 'Then why do the wheels of their wagons not leave deeper ruts in the earth as they become more and more heavy with the many skins they carry?'

'I think it is because they use the same wagons for carrying the hides that they use for transporting their provisions,' answered Walks-Like-A-Shadow immediatedly. 'So, as they use up their boxes of ammunition and food supplies at a certain rate then the wagons become lighter. But, as they load them with hides at a similar rate, the weight does not change much. Do you not consider it possible?'

The others nodded in silent assent.

'And do you not also agree that there is but one way to discover whether I am right in what I feel – and that is to get close enough to them to see what is in their wagons?'

Again, his two friends nodded.

'Then, there can be only one way to accomplish this without being discovered ourselves,' he continued. 'We will do it at night under a blanket of darkness. Tonight I think. While it is still daylight, however, we will move in as close as we can to make it but a short journey after the sun has left the sky. We must keep clear of them just as they kept clear of the buffalo. To avoid being heard or smelt by the buffalo, the hunters circled them and then moved in close with the wind blowing towards them and not towards the buffalo. We will do the same.'

The three Kiowas never once relaxed their vigilance as they encircled the hunters and moved in behind their camp.

While it was still light they studied its layout with meticulous care. They also had time to witness the wanton slaughter of the buffalo. Their buffalo. The buffalo of the Plains Indians. They watched as the white men spread-eagled themselves downwind of the lumbering herds, placed the barrels of their long, heavy buffalo guns in the notches of forked sticks planted firmly into the ground, carefully adjusted the sights of their weapons and then commenced shooting down the huge beasts with cold-blooded accuracy. It was a massacre that did not stop until the last animal of each herd had either been killed or run away.

The three copper-hued witnesses of this savage mass murder of countless hundreds of buffalo which could have fed, clothed and housed entire Indian tribes, kept silent only by exercising the greatest self-control. Each of them fought down, and then only with the utmost difficulty, the almost irresistible urge to fire their rifles at the American hunters until they had no more bullets left with which to kill these ruthless white men.

# Chapter Eight

The hunters had a leader. He was a tall man dressed, like his men, in filthy clothes spattered with great blotches of blood and grease. Although the Kiowas could not hear with any clarity what he said, it was obvious that everyone he spoke to did just as the big man indicated with a jerk of his thumb, a nod of his head or the pointing of a solitary finger. Most of the time his back was towards the three young warriors. But just once he turned in their direction and they could see his rugged, tanned face with its drooping moustache.

A single audible involuntary gasp came from between the lips of Walks-Like-Shadow before he had the time to even think about attempting to stifle it. 'Quilter!' he breathed in a shocked whisper.

The two other braves turned to look at their friend. His face clearly displayed a look of murderous hatred such as neither of them had ever seen him show before. His flint-hard eyes were fixed firmly upon the tall man directing the hunters. Had the white man not been responsible for the slaughter of so many buffalo, Mountain Cat and Short Legs could have felt sorry for him. They dared not speak to Walks-Like-A-Shadow at that moment for fear of betraying themselves to the Americans. But, as soon as the opportunity arose, they would have many questions to ask him.

The three of them continued to lie there in absolute silence. All the suspicions of Walks-Like-A-Shadow had been confirmed. Yet they must still wait for nightfall.

As soon as the echo of the final gunshot, that sped on its way the bullet which downed the last animal of that particular herd, faded into nothing, the buffalo hunters laid aside their weapons and staggered to their feet. Their faces were black with powder burns and they swayed on their benumbed legs. Their shoulders and hands ached painfully from hours of virtually non-stop shooting.

But as their task finished so that of the buffalo skinners began. Each team of two men tackled one animal after another with an almost unbelievable swiftness. First they used their razor-sharp knives to slit open the underside of the hide along the beast's belly and the insides of its four legs. Then the skin was attached by a rope to a horse which was urged forward until the hide was ripped clear of the carcase. Then the skin was pegged to the ground, inside uppermost, and left to dry. The area surrounding the Americans was soon covered with almost countless hides.

The three warriors could have slipped away at this point but for one thing. They still had to find out for what purpose the buffalo pelts were required and why in such vast quantities. To even attempt to uncover this mystery it would be necessary for Walks-Like-A-Shadow, with his knowledge of the white man's language, to steal in close to their camp after dark and learn what he could from the Americans' conversations. Food, liquor and a warm fire soon loosened men's tongues, no matter what their race.

As darkness fell so fires began to spring up throughout

the camp. As the three warriors had stationed themselves downwind, the smell of cooking soon reminded them of their empty stomachs. However, they continued to lie in silent agony as from the encampment below drifted not only the odours of stewing, frying and grilling, but also the clatter of metal against metal as the Americans filled their plates and started eating. The white men ate noisily and the air was soon filled with the sounds of their hearty appetites at work, interspersed with lusty belching and laughter. Then came the popping of corks, the gurgle of whisky into cups and the beginnings of relaxed, if somewhat raucous, conversation.

Walks-Like-A-Shadow motioned to his two companions that he intended moving in closer to the buffalo killers in order to hear more clearly the things about which they talked. He knew that, inevitably, they would make some reference to the buffalo hides for they, obviously, were the sole reason for the presence of the white hunters. And he had noticed earlier the intense excitement in their eyes as they had ruthlessly and methodically slaughtered an entire herd by shooting at them from all angles so that there was no direction in which the panic-stricken animals could run in order to escape death from the heavy calibre bullets. It was a total massacre. Not one buffalo had emerged alive from the murderous cross-fire of the Americans' guns. So, sooner or later, if he waited long enough, there would be words among them about these skins which were so important to them. Of this he was certain.

Quilter had posted armed men around the camp perimeter but they merely played at being sentries. These were careless men who paid attention only to those distractions in progress around the fires within the area they were supposed to guard. Some of them were even singing or humming to the melodies being played on a battered harmonica by an equally battered old-timer seated close to one of the fires. It was but child's play for Walks-Like-A-Shadow to snake his way noiselessly through the undergrowth and long coarse grass, slithering past the guards until he was sufficiently near to the centre of the encampment to hear clearly all that was said.

'Clem, that meal you cooked was just about your worst yet,' complained a man seated so close to Walks-Like-A-Shadow that he could have stretched out his arm and almost touched him. 'And you sure as hellfire have served up some rough ones on this trail.'

'You don't like my cooking then that's okay by me sonny. All you got to do is cook your own from here on in.'

'Oh I would sure enough but for one thing.'

'What's that?'

'My cooking tastes a helluva sight lousier at its best than yours at its worst.'

This produced guffaws of laughter with the heartiest coming from the man named Clem. 'Gotta be honest with you all,' he said as the laughter subsided. 'Back home buffalo tongues was a big luxury in eating houses. And I heard also that they cost a fortune in dude restaurants in the East. But right now I'd swap buffalo tongue, buffalo ribs or any other damn cut of buffalo for a juicy beef steak.'

'You know your trouble Clem?' interrupted another hunter.

'No, what's that?'

'You think too much about buffalo meat and not

enough about their hides. Your mind's got its roots in your belly instead of your pockets.'

'That's right,' agreed yet another man. 'Once we finished this hunt you'll have enough cash to buy all the beefsteaks you can eat.'

'And all the whisky and women you want as well,' added someone else.

'No women for me,' remarked the grizzled veteran who had been playing the harmonica but had now chosen to join in the conversation. 'At my age whisky and good eating is more than enough for any man.'

'Hell, you old buzzard, what do you need the beefsteaks and liquor for if it ain't to build up your strength and put you in the right mood for a good woman?' queried someone from the other side of the fire around which this particular group, the nearest to where Walks-Like-A-Shadow lay in concealment, was seated.

'Well, to tell you the truth sonny boy,' replied the old man, 'After I finishes one of them big juicy steaks you all been talking about I always fancies me a woman. The bigger the better. Then I starts to have a drink or two to get me in just the right frame of mind to tackle one just like I fancies. Then it happens.'

'What does?' came the chorus from his companions whose sexual appetites were thoroughly aroused by now.

'Well,' drawled the old man, 'Fact is that by the time my insides is all aglow with all that whisky I been drinking, I clean forget what it was that made me start drinking to get in the right mood for.'

Bellows of laughter greeted his words. The old-timer sucked on the stem of an ancient pipe he had pulled from a pocket in his jacket. 'Hell, it ain't such a bad old

94

world,' he told himself contentedly. 'Not when you can make youngsters like these laugh, enjoy a pipe of baccy, a decent meal and still feel the pleasant sensation brought on by downing a few whiskies.'

As the laughter died down the youngest member of the group, a surly-faced fair-haired boy still in his late teens, grumbled, 'What I can't understand is why we don't quit now, get our share of cash and enjoy some good living. I'm sick of all this rotten stink. Surely we got enough buffalo pelts already?'

'You must be joking boy,' commented the man called Clem. 'Don't you hear good? When we first set out Quilter said we was going to follow the buffalo until there was none left along the trail he picked. And you got to admit boy, Quilter sure picked one Godalmighty money-packed trail. Just look at all the hides we got already. And we all know there's still a helluva lot more ahead of us.'

'Then why can't we leave 'em until another time?' moaned the fair-haired youngster.

'Because there might not be another time.' The voice was that of Quilter himself. He had been strolling through the camp when the boy's questions reached his ears. 'We have to follow these critters until there's none left in this part of the country. Then we'll trade 'em in and start looking elsewhere for some more.'

In his place of concealment Walks-Like-A-Shadow could feel his stomach churning. With great difficulty he fought down an almost uncontrollable desire to leap up and shoot Quilter. But he knew that such an action would achieve nothing other than the death of one man. The rest of the hunters would still continue killing the buffalo. And, in addition, they would have been warned that the Indian tribes were aware of what the white men were doing. This would only make the hunters much more vigilant – and dangerous, for they were all formidable shots.

The boy turned towards Quilter. 'What's the hurry?' he asked in a sullen tone. 'The buffalo will still be around when we come back. We need a break from all this. It's only fair.'

Quilter placed his right hand on the youngster's left shoulder and squeezed hard. The boy groaned in pain, but Quilter paid no attention. Instead, he kept up the pressure and told him, 'Nothing's fair in this life son and you'd better learn that fast or you won't survive long. Of course the buffalo will still be here next time round – if other hunters don't get to them first. But, with hides fetching the prices they do, it's a case of first come, first served. Now can you tell me of anyone stupid enough to pass up a chance of rich pickings just so as to wait for a man called Quilter and his boys to come back when they feel like it and carry on where they left off? Can you sonny?'

The boy's eyes were moist. He shook his head. The hand on his shoulder tightened its grip. 'No Mr Quilter,' he gasped in pain.

'That's better. Learning sense already.' Quilter took his hand from the youngster's shoulder and patted him on the head. 'Just leave the thinking to your betters sonny. Listen and learn. You'll live a lot longer and richer that way.'

Quilter paused, took a cheroot from his pocket, placed it between his lips, snatched a burning twig from the fire, lit the cheroot and inhaled slowly. 'Another thing we have to consider is whether them factories in the East will go on using buffalo hides for machine belting or look for something cheaper.'

'Such as?' queried the grizzled old-timer.

'How should I know,' replied Quilter. 'Cow hides I shouldn't be surprised. No, whatever way you look at it, we just got to make all we can while we can. When the bottom falls out of the market is the time to quit. Not before.' Inhaling deeply on his cheroot, he turned slowly on his heel and continued his walk through the encampment.

His words left Walks-Like-A-Shadow a puzzled man. He knew not the meanings of the terms 'factories' and 'machine belting'. But he did know that Quilter, and men like him, would kill all the buffalo, the Plains Indians' only means of survival, unless they were stopped.

Without pausing to reason the possible consequences of the impulses that now radiated from his fury-filled mind, the Kiowa glided silently after Quilter. One thought blocked all others. And that thought was kill, kill, kill.

But a man so possessed by uncontrolled anger often makes mistakes. Walks-Like-A-Shadow, knife in hand ready for a quiet kill so as not to arouse Quilter's compatriots, stepped on a dry, brittle twig just as he was about to plunge the weapon upwards into the army deserter's back so that it pierced his heart from behind.

The twig snapped with a sound like that made when a child fires a cap pistol. Quilter swung round with incredible speed and moved instinctively to one side. The blade intended for his heart left a furrow along his left cheek where he had just failed to jerk back far enough to avoid its razor-sharp point.

In an instant he recognised Walks-Like-A-Shadow and

bellowed like a lanced bull in a Mexican ring. 'It's that son-of-a-bitch Kiowa!' he shouted. 'Stop him someone!'

But he was too late. Walks-Like-A-Shadow ran like a deer. His thoughts were no longer distorted by the killing lust that had possessed him minutes earlier. And with a clear mind, his natural abilities and an unrivalled knowledge of his environment, no white man, and very few red men, could even hope to catch him. Covered by the cloak of friendly darkness, he soon joined his two friends.

For several minutes they lay flat against the earth beneath them so that none of the bullets being discharged wildly in all directions by the panic-stricken hunters, convinced that they were facing a full-scale Indian attack, hit them by accident.

'You stupid bastard, you almost blasted my backside to kingdom come! Point that bloody shotgun some other way!' The irate shouting of the incensed hunter, whoever he was, brought a lull in the firing and a degree of sanity, plus a few belly laughs, to the camp.

So no one had difficulty in hearing when Quilter's voice bellowed: 'Stop shooting for Christ's sake! It's just one lousy Indian. He's clear gone by now. You scared him witless – as well as each other.'

But as the men returned from the darkness to the firelit centre of the camp, the three Kiowas could hear Quilter ordering out guards for the night. Judging by the number of names he called he was taking no risks that Walks-Like-A-Shadow might still remain close by.

The three Kiowas rose from their hiding place, returned to their ponies and began the long ride back to Fort Sill.

# Chapter Nine

When Walks-Like-A-Shadow, Short Legs and Mountain Cat were still almost two miles distant from the fort they could see a diminutive figure on horseback galloping towards them. It was several minutes before they recognised the rider to be a woman. But only a few seconds more passed before Walks-Like-A-Shadow realised it was Summer Cloud. He left his two companions to follow on as he urged his weary mount to one last burst of speed. The pony, sensing they were nearing home and rest, responded superbly.

The heart of Walks-Like-A-Shadow pounded almost in time with his horse's hoofbeats as he saw clearly the eager smile upon Summer Cloud's face. She was a splendid horsewoman and the muscles of the magnificent palamino pony she rode rippled like those of a well-trained athlete as she rapidly closed the gap that still separated her from the oncoming warrior she loved so deeply.

As she reined her mount to a sharp halt, leaving its glossy golden-brown flanks heaving and quivering from the sudden unaccustomed exertion following the lethargy of winter and early spring, turned it gracefully around and rode alongside Walks-Like-A-Shadow, she could see that he was much marked by the hardships of long, arduous travel and practically asleep in the saddle from extreme exhaustion. But she was so happy and relieved that her man was otherwise unhurt. Ever since Bull Shoulders and the others had returned to the village, laden with the results of a successful buffalo hunt and explained what the three missing warriors had set out to accomplish, she had nursed a growing fear that Walks-Like-A-Shadow had either been killed by the men they followed or, at best, seriously wounded. She tried hard to hide her anxiety from the man who now turned towards her and showed unashamedly in his eyes the deep feelings he felt for his woman.

'Well, my handsome and hard-working husband what beautiful maiden from which tribe kept you away from home for so long?' she teased, her beautiful dark eyes twinkling with mischief. The humour that comes so naturally with real love and the deep trust that accompanies it, is not a monopoly possessed only by white people. It is universal wherever men and women are free to love as they wish those with whom they share their mutual desires.

Walks-Like-A-Shadow knew she was playing with him and, tired though he was, decided to join in the game. The expression of tenderness upon his face swiftly became one of guilt and anger. 'What makes you say such things woman?' he thundered. 'Can a man not be away from his wife for any length of time without her becoming suspicious? Who told you about my other woman? Come on, tell me!'

Her look of happiness at seeing her husband returning to the village unharmed after so many days away, now changed to one of absolute dejection and disbelief. In fact she appeared so downcast that Walks-Like-A-Shadow could not prevent himself from bellowing with laughter.

Summer Cloud looked up at him with a mixture of

relief and mock anger intermingled upon her features. 'What kind of wickedness is this that makes you torment in this manner the woman who loves you so dearly and is so filled with joy that you have returned to her unhurt?'

'The same kind of wickedness that makes you playfully accuse your husband, who experienced feelings of love equally as great as your own when you rode towards him just now, of unfaithfulness with another woman,' softly replied Walks-Like-A-Shadow. 'Now we are even in this game you started. Or do you wish to play more?'

'Of course I wish to play with you more my husband.' Her voice was as gentle as her name and the sparkle had returned to her eyes. 'But not this game. I had another one in mind. One that only a man and a woman can play when they are alone with no one else in sight to distract them.'

Walks-Like-A-Shadow suddenly sat straight in his saddle, all traces of tiredness rapidly disappearing from his powerful body. 'This game is one I feel I will like very much indeed. As soon as we have told our story to the tribal elders I will come to you in our tepee, eat a good meal, for I think I will need much strength, and then we will play your game together. The loser will be the person who falls asleep first.'

'I fear that will be you my husband for we have been long apart and I have rested well,' said Summer Cloud contentedly.

'We shall see,' murmured Walks-Like-A-Shadow as he caressed soothingly the smooth red-brown arm of the woman riding alongside him. 'We shall see. And I suspect that there will be great fun in the finding out.'

As Mountain Cat and Short Legs drew level, the four

of them hastened their flagging horses towards the many buffalo-skin lodges spread out across the land before them. For the three warriors it felt good to be so close to their homes again. For the woman it felt good to be so close to her husband again.

They rode into the camp to a triumphant welcome. Bull Shoulders, once more his amicable self, had been informed of their return by scouts he had sent out. His hunt had been good and many buffalo had been killed.

Like all Indians, the Kiowas loved to eat and dance. They required only the slightest excuse for an all night celebration. The home-coming of the three warriors was a massive excuse. So, forewarned of this safe return, a feast was being prepared to suit the importance of the occasion.

Walks-Like-A-Shadow and his companions, Short Legs and Mountain Cat, soon forgot their exhaustion and looked forward with eager anticipation to the celebrations planned for that night at which they would be guests of honour.

There was much laughter and activity in the village. It was like earlier times in the tribe's history – and not so far back that they had been obscured by the mists which soon envelop the past. Times when the region abounded with buffalo and white men were few. Few because their leaders had mistakenly labelled the Southern Plains on their maps as The Great American Desert because of the intense dry summer heat and the apparent infinity coupled with a sparseness of timber.

Yet the Kiowa mood that day was an illusion. They were surrounded by white soldiers. For the Americans had soon discovered the truth. The vast treeless spaces of Texas and its neighbouring territories were not all areas of desert. Far from it, in fact. In most instances, the expanses of land previously called desert by the whites were swiftly and surely discovered to be gigantic grasslands capable of sustaining equally colossal herds of cattle.

So, once the land-hungry Americans found that fortunes could be made by grazing the Southern Plains, the five nomadic tribes who called the region their home simply had to go. But where? The United States government was still working on that problem.

Walks-Like-A-Shadow felt like a person split down the middle. Although he had become infected to a degree by the enthusiasm of the Kiowas around him, it had not yet developed into the acute state of euphoria which seemed to have the overwhelming majority of his fellow villagers firmly within its grasp.

No, Walks-Like-A-Shadow was aware of the illusion. He knew what was happening out on the plains while the people around him prepared for a night of feasting and dancing. The buffalo were being slaughtered mercilessly in thousands. Perhaps in tens of thousands even; or greater still. The Kiowa, the Comanche and the other tribes had to be forced to acknowledge the wholesale massacre of the teeming herds before it was too late. Without the buffalo, around which the entire lives of the Southern Plains Indians revolved, they must die also. For where else could they go? What else could they do?

No, a world without buffalo would mean the end of the Kiowas. He had to find Satanta, Satank and the other tribal leaders and discuss this thing with them. They would have an answer. There had to be one. The only alternatives to a land where there were no more buffalo were either death or the ways of the white man.

He knew the whites would never accept the Indians as equals so his thoughts turned to death. He was not afraid of dying. Yet he would not welcome it either. Before it took him, as it did everyone eventually, he would fight against death with all his strength and energy until, weakened by the battle itself, he would lose. But never without a fight. Life was a series of experiences yet to be encountered. A series of challenges. He was a fighting man. He wanted to meet all these things. Life was good for a warrior. Too good to surrender it without the toughest of struggles. All these thoughts fluttered into his mind and out again as he searched the bustling encampment for Satanta.

Eventually he found the chief. He was with Bull Shoulders. Both men were thoroughly drunk. Their glazed eyes failed even to recognise him. He turned and strode away in disgust. But it would not end here. It was far too important to them all. He would speak with Satanta tomorrow. Hangover or not, he would make the chief listen.

The following day dawned clear and soon developed that fierce heat experienced only by places such as the vast grasslands of the south. The cloudless blue sky was flawless apart from a solitary white-hot disc that relentlessly bounced its searing heat waves against the earth beneath. In similar circumstances on such days most nomadic peoples the world over feel a glowing contentment within themselves, particularly when they have eaten well, have more food ready to hand and nothing other than a time of leisurely pursuits ahead of them. For, if ever a day was created for little else other than simply lazing around then this was just such a one.

Yet this was not the case in the Kiowa camp that morning. Instead of smiles most faces wore heavy scowls. Some were even distorted by grimaces of pain. The still air, for the restless prairie winds seemed to have taken the day off, was filled with groans of varying pitches and of different duration. Most men, and many women also, staggered from their lodges with their eyes tightly closed against the sun's pitiless glare and their hands covering their faces for added protection from its probing, unremitting rays.

'Ai-yee!' exclaimed Satanta as he crawled through the opening of his hot, airless tepee only to be greeted by those same sledgehammer blows from the fiery furnace above. 'My head is bursting with the sound of drums,' he moaned. 'And my stomach feels as if it is carrying a great sickness.'

'The only sickness inside you and these other poor fools is that caused by too much whisky,' said an unsympathetic voice beside him. It was Walks-Like-A-Shadow. He and others like him who had not spent the previous night drinking heavily were enjoying greatly the obvious discomfort of those who had. 'I have seen you take knife and bullet wounds that could not bring you to your knees like this.'

Satanta turned his neck to look upwards, shielding his eyes from the sun and attempting to focus them on the man who dared address him thus. 'So it is you,' he grunted at the young warrior. 'Do you have to be so right? Cannot an old man enjoy a single failing? Or do you expect him to be forever perfect because accident has made him chief.'

'You are not a chief by accident,' retorted Walks-Like-A-Shadow. 'You struggled against many hardships and enemies to become a leader of your people. They need you – but not like this.'

'What have I done to deserve a conscience like you?' growled Satanta. 'There is enough noise inside my head without your added chatter coming from outside it.' He forced himself into a sitting position. 'If you must lecture me then at least come down to my level so to do. For I do not yet trust my legs sufficiently to keep me standing upright while I trade insults with you.' He sighed as Walks-Like-A-Shadow sat down beside him. He had hoped that this particular pain would walk off and permit him to recover in comparative peace from those which would not leave him so easily. 'So be it,' he grunted. 'Start your lecture.'

'There is no need. You will do that yourself when you are completely sober again.'

'Then, if you are not here to grumble about my over-indulgence, what do you want with me?'

'To speak of our people and their future if there is such a thing ahead of them. To tell you of what Short Legs, Mountain Cat and I discovered while Bull Shoulders and the others were hunting buffalo.'

Satanta sobered considerably as he heard the other's words and the serious manner in which he spoke. 'You were not here merely by chance when I came out,' he stated. 'You were waiting for me. Are these things you have to tell me that important?'

'They are,' replied Walks-Like-A-Shadow.

'Well, tell me then!' demanded a more thoroughly awake and extremely impatient Satanta as he straightened his back and looked much more like the powerful chief he was.

'My words are hard for there is no way I can soften

them. Our buffalo are being slaughtered by white men. We watched them at their savage and senseless butchery after following the stench-ridden trail of many thousands of rotting buffalo carcases across a great distance to find out who was killing them. Had anyone told me of what was happening and had I not seen it for myself I would have found it almost impossible to believe. But I have seen it and it is true.'

Satanta sat motionless, staring at the far off horizon. He had the look of a man in another world; a place that no other person could ever enter with him. 'So that is how they will do it,' he said almost to himself after several minutes of silence. 'Kill the buffalo and the spirit of the people will die with them.'

'This is what will happen if we do not stop them,' agreed his young companion. 'But this is not their intention.'

'What makes you say this?'

'I say it because I crept in close enough to hear the white hunters say that they were selling the buffalo hides in the east for much money.'

'So they were not just killing them to bring us to submission but for their skins,' commented Satanta. 'No matter what the reason, the end will be the same if these butchers are not stopped. Our people in stockades begging for food like the white man's sheep and cattle. Such a thing would be worse than death. That they could conquer us by killing our buffalo is something that had never once occurred to me I must confess.'

'Or to me before I saw how easily and quickly such massive slaughters can be achieved,' admitted Walks-Like-A-Shadow.

'But how do we stop them? Perhaps the killing will

cease when they have all the buffalo skins they want.'

'Perhaps. But how many is enough for them? Remember, this is the only spring when we have not found buffalo on the first day of the chase. So their numbers must already be much fewer than before. No, we cannot even hope that they will stop killing them. Such thoughts must never be considered a possible answer to such a terrible problem. The white men must be stopped. There is no other way.'

'But how do we stop them? If we fight them on their terms we can only lose. Our people cannot take the losses as the white men can. We are encumbered by our women and children. They are not. And every time we kill a white soldier it seems that ten more take his place. There is a great difference between raiding and all-out war. The first is a way of life for the Kiowas but the second can only be a way of death.'

Walks-Like-A-Shadow nodded his head in agreement. 'This is so. But if we are forced to make a choice between living their way or dying our way then I think many of us will prefer to die with dignity than live with dishonour.'

Satanta remained silent and motionless, staring far into the distance. He was once again in his other place where no person could reach him. His face wore a look of a man almost without hope. Walks-Like-A-Shadow rose quietly and moved softly away. Perhaps Satanta could find an answer before returning from his other world. Who could tell? He doubted it. But, whatever, there were hard times ahead for the Kiowas. Of that there was no doubt.

Yet the days that followed brought no further signs of anything other than the normal difficulties which faced the red men of the Southern Plains every spring. Even

Satanta's dark moods were replaced by optimism as the days grew longer and entered that time of the year which the white men called summer. Admittedly the buffalo, wherever they were found, were in far smaller herds than in previous years and hunting parties had to be far more frequent and travel much greater distances than before. But, nevertheless, the people's stomachs had as much buffalo meat in them as during times past. Their earlier troubles of that year were soon forgotten. This was the way of the Kiowas. And there was even a look about them which said clearly that life was good once more for the tribe.

By the time the sun had climbed to its highest point of the year even the most pessimistic among them grudgingly conceded that life was as pleasant as during those times which preceded the coming of the white men – well, almost as good. So no-one was much surprised when Satanta called them together one day and told them what they had already been feeling and even discussing.

'But do you know why life is once more as it was?' he asked them. 'Do you know why the soldiers no longer come among us looking for fights?' A smugness settled upon his features as he observed much shaking of heads. A quietness reached out across those around him. Satanta still loved to make speeches. But he needed attentive audiences and, wise leader that he was, he knew that here he had one clasped firmly in his hand. He savoured the situation. This is much better than even the finest whisky, he told himself.

'Well, I will tell you why the white people are now leaving us alone.' He paused in order to allow his words to create the impact they undoubtedly would among a people renowned for their curiosity. Soon he was rewarded with the absolute silence he knew would come. No orator anywhere enjoyed more than Satanta did to hold an audience thus. But he knew just how long he could keep total attention upon himself without losing it to individual speculations of what was to come so he did not make them wait beyond that moment. 'The white people's leader in Washington wants peace with the Indian nations,' he boomed.

Hundreds of voices started talking at once. He relished the moment and waited for the chatter to subside. As the tongues slowly stilled one man could be heard clearly above the people around him. 'They are afraid of us!', he said loudly and triumphantly. 'Have not I, Bull Shoulders, always said this would happen? They do not have the strong hearts of our warriors.'

'If you believe that then you are a fool,' commented Short Legs from somewhere behind him.

'Little man with his big mouth has more muscles in his tongue than in the rest of his body,' scoffed Bull Shoulders. 'I think that. . . .'

'You cannot think,' retorted Short Legs. 'You have never had a thought in your whole life. If you were lucky enough to have an idea you would not know what to do with it. It would give you a headache.'

Bull Shoulders raised his massive frame upright and started to push his way through the packed figures surrounding him. 'This time I will squeeze your tongue until it is as small as your legs,' he growled.

Short Legs leaped to his feet. He hated any reference to his under-sized lower limbs and his eyes blazed angrily as he moved towards Bull Shoulders.

But Walks-Like-A-Shadow, fortunately, was seated

between them and he too stood up. 'Both of you sit down and close your mouths tightly. I am a friend to both of you. Yet, whoever attacks the other then I will help the one who is assaulted. Your behaviour insults one of our most respected tribal elders. Your shame is our shame for are we not all Kiowas?' Bull Shoulders and Short Legs immediatedly seated themselves upon the ground again. Both wore expressions of guilt but there was also murder smouldering deep within the eyes of the bigger man. Walks-Like-A-Shadow also returned to his place on the earth.

Satanta waited for all the muttering around him to die down before continuing. 'The white men now have a new leader. He is called General Grant. He says he knows his soldiers can defeat our warriors in war for he has more men and much better weapons. These last things at least are true as we know. And they do not have their women and children among them during battles. There is no danger to their families for they remain behind whenever the soldiers come. But we cannot do this for our people live as one family and our women and children are more often killed than our fighting men in such battles.

'President Grant has decided to try for peace between his people and ours because some white medicine men, called Quakers, have asked him to do this thing. These Quakers are men of peace who do not like war and if they are powerful enough to get their leader to do as they wish then they must also be strong men. Remember that President Grant is also a general so it would seem that among white people not all men of strength and power are warriors. These Quakers are not fighting men and yet they must be brave. For, not only do they cause this leader Grant to change from war to peace, but they are also sending their Quaker men of peace to become agents among Indians everywhere. The man who is coming to be our agent is called Tatum.'

# Chapter Ten

Lawrie Tatum was a middle-aged Quaker farmer from Iowa. He was an honest, sincere, enthusiastic and fearless man with one formidable ambition – to turn the seasoned warriors who were now his charges into peaceful farmers. He took over from Colonel Hazen on July 1st. Agent Tatum realised that the height of summer was not at all the ideal time to start attempting to convert carefree, far-ranging nomads – with all that they needed free for the taking throughout the endless prairies they called home – into fenced-in agricultural workers. But he was determined to succeed. 'I will give 500 dollars each year to be divided among the ten Indians who raise the best crops,' he told a meeting of their leaders.

Tatum even organised the purchase of sawmill equipment, a steam engine and a shingling machine to assist the tribes with their farming endeavours. And he was encouraged by the early results of his efforts. The Indians, who respected the agent's courage, honesty and justice, started to plant and cultivate vegetables, corn and melons.

However, on a tour of inspection one day, he was enraged when he saw that practically all the work was being done by the women. He ranted at the men after seeking them out and finding the great majority of them in far more leisurely pursuits. 'You can't leave your women to do the work!' he raved at Satanta when he found him indulging in gambling games with several of his cronies.

'Why not?' replied the chief calmly as he looked up from squatting on his hunches with his fellow gamblers. 'Farming is women's work.'

'It may well have been so in the past but not now,' argued Tatum mopping his perspiring bald head with a yellow kerchief with black polka dots. He was feeling irritable. To be honest he was extremely edgy. It was infernally hot and he was both thirsty and hungry after riding in the dry heat for what seemed endless hours.

'It will always be women's work,' answered an unperturbed Satanta as he continued gambling with his friends – this time with a game involving sticks of different lengths. 'It was never intended for men to become women.'

By now the agent was almost at boiling point. His face was changing to deeper shades of red by the second. Normally a baby pink, with patches of it left peeling by the boiling sun, it was soon a deep crimson occasioned by both heat and anger – the former uncontrollable and the latter almost so. 'Then, what in God's name, is your role in tribal life?' thundered Tatum, his black-spotted yellow kerchief working overtime as the beads of sweat glistening on his bald dome quickly became rivulets of perspiration streaming downwards from all directions into the gap between his neck and the collar surrounding it.

'Me?' queried Satanta, this time a little more cautiously. 'I am chief. You know it. So why do you ask me?'

A glint leaped into the agent's eyes and seemed to spark off an explosion. 'Not you!' he roared.

'Then who?' asked a puzzled Satanta now on his feet, backing slowly and apprehensively away. He was accompanied by his companions who had also risen in accord with the increase in the volume of wrath emanating from their erstwhile friend and benefactor whose normally placid pink features were now redder than those of his red charges.

The roar became an ear-shattering bellow. 'I mean all of you! Not just you, you ... you simpleton. I mean all the men of the tribe! What part in creation do you all think you are intended for?'

A totally nonplussed Satanta was delighted when Walks-Like-A-Shadow, hearing without difficulty from some distance away all that the agent had poured forth, rode over to interpret those words which were becoming increasingly incomprehensible to his chief. Satanta's English was improving – but much too slowly to deal with Tatum's verbal eruption. However, after the young Kiowa had finished his translation, the chief was no longer delighted. He looked in anger at Tatum who was still fuming visibly.

'You know without asking what the men of all Indian tribes are for,' Satanta told him, an ominous edge now evident in his tone. 'We are for hunting and war. That is how it has been with us for all time. We cannot change now and become women. And if we could we would not. Your president can make us do many things for he has more soldiers than the prairies have blades of grass. But he cannot take away our manhood. For us it would be easier to die. Much easier. You hear me Tatum?'

'Yes I hear you.' The agent's words were slower and

easier to understand for he had succeeded in regaining control of his emotions. 'But there is no longer any need for you to be warriors or hunters. There is to be no more fighting and all the meat you require for your people will come from the livestock raised on your own farms.'

'We will never do women's work!' stated Satanta emphatically as he turned and strode away from Tatum. All but Walks-Like-A-Shadow followed him. The young warrior turned towards the downcast white man who now knew he could never truly be the leader of these Indians.

The agent's anger had now turned to a resigned depression. He looked at Walks-Like-A-Shadow. 'What can I do?' he asked dejectedly. 'I want them to stay alive. To lead useful lives. That is my responsibility. That is why I chose to come here. The Indians can never win a war against the United States. We all know that.'

The young warrior gazed steadily at Tatum. 'Do you think that Satanta and the rest do not understand how it is. I know you mean good for them. But you must understand that to them life means different things than it does to the white man. White men fear death most. Not so with Indians. To us there are many things worse than death. For the Kiowas and other Indian warriors to be deprived of their right to be men – to hunt and to fight for their people – is the most bad thing that can happen to them. They would be much happier to die fighting than to surrender this right. Believe me agent Tatum.' His voice dropped to almost a whisper. 'Believe me or you can only fail.'

Tatum moved uneasily and uncomfortably in his suddenly sticky but rock-hard saddle as Walks-Like-A-Shadow wheeled his mount and rode off in the direction taken by the others. Tatum sighed audibly. Where had he erred? It had all seemed so straightforward and uncomplicated when he first accepted the post. He had even looked forward to the challenge. But now? He sighed again and looked up at the heavens. No divine revelations for this servant of the Lord, he mused despondently as he turned his eyes back down to face the bleak horizon. Nothing but bleakness ahead in more ways than one, he thought. He reined his horse's head gently around and kneed it slowly forward in the direction of the agency. Speed came with enthusiasm or fear. Right now he knew neither.

Upon his return to the post the news that awaited him did nothing to alleviate his despair. In fact it caused his despondency to plunge to even greater depths. Big Bow and his small band of Kiowas who, together with the Quohada branch of the Comanches continued to range the Staked Plains and refused to come in for rations, had started to taunt all those Indians who had agreed to reside within the environs of Fort Sill. They had even sent a messenger to Tatum in person to tell him that they would never shake hands with him and accept him as their agent, not even if the pony soldiers rode to the Indians' homes dotted across the plains and beat them into submission. And that was never likely to happen, added the messenger before leaping back astride his horse and galloping rapidly away in the direction of the Staked Plains.

But, contrary to Tatum's expectations, the other Kiowas and Comanches remained more or less within the reservation boundaries and maintained an uneasy truce with the agent. Wisely he refrained, for the time being at least, making any further serious issue of the farming situation. He referred to it casually from time to time but decided that now was not the time for ultimatums. Sometimes it paid to let the pot simmer for a while. Thrusting your fingers into its boiling contents generally left you with nothing other than a painfully scalded hand.

As the summer slowly but inevitably surrendered its greener hues to the limitless shades of brown, red, orange and yellow that announced the arrival of autumn to the southern grasslands, so Tatum's depression began to lift. And, as the trees began to shed their foliage so the agent likewise succeeded in shrugging off the final vestiges of his earlier despondency.

The government regarded Tatum's agency as a successful example to be displayed by the president as a vindication of his peace policy to those politicians who still doubted the wisdom of his employing Quakers to tackle a task that had defeated their numerous predecessors. To be truthful the agent quite enjoyed the glory that came his way. Of course both he and Satanta knew who was really in charge of the situation but the chief never bragged of it. He liked things just the way they were. It was simply a game that suited its two player-captains. Even being on the losing side had its compensations, reflected Tatum. But he knew it was only a temporary arrangement. He had convinced himself he would really tackle his Indian problem . . . one day.

And the situation might just have remained thus until the two main participants had learned a little more about one another and the moves that each was likely to make in any given set of circumstances. Then, by correct mutual understanding and manipulation of the pieces on the board, the game could have developed into a pleasant, long-running contest destined some time far hence to end in an equally pleasant stalemate.

However, albeit unwittingly, the military decided to join in the fun. And, against all the rules concocted and accepted to date by Tatum and Satanta, the militia cheated. The chief immediately resigned and never forgave his opponents.

The army, represented by a mere handful of soldiers with a misplaced sense of humour and a disastrous sense of timing, made its opening – and closing – move in the game during the winter of that year.

The move started innocently enough when Satanta, always on the look-out for a free drink, spotted an almost full liquor bottle standing unattended and invitingly uncorked on a bench outside the fort stables. He grabbed it by the neck and took a long, powerful swig. Too powerful, it so happened, because the bottle contained an evil-tasting liquid which had been dispensed to treat a sick mule – and externally at that. A few seconds after returning the bottle quickly to the bench, in the hope that no one had seen him sneaking a drink, Satanta sent forth a mighty roar and clasped his hands across his stomach now seized with agonising pains. Bent almost double, he stumbled over to the nearby officers' quarters begging for medicine to dispel his suffering.

By now some of the soldiers grouped idly around that particular part of the fort were smiling broadly. Word had reached them of Satanta's discomfort, and the reason for it, via a stage driver who had witnessed all that had occurred.

At first the officer who eventually opened the door of his quarters in answer to Satanta's persistent pounding and bellowing refused to give him anything to ease his agony. Then the officer noticed one of the grinning soldiers pointing first to the bottle outside the stables and then at the Kiowa chief. Quick to assess the situation the officer decided to play a joke upon Satanta. Suppressing a grin with the greatest difficulty, he walked over to a cupboard situated a few paces inside the entrance to his quarters. Taking out a bottle of the most nauseating medicine he could find he pretended to drink from it before returning the bottle to the cupboard and leaving the room.

Immediately he had gone Satanta rushed across to the cupboard, grabbed the bottle and poured the contents down his throat. 'Eo-ow!' he screamed as his entire chest seemed suddenly crammed with red hot coals. There were tears of pain in his eyes as he blundered through the soldiers surrounding him. They, and the officer who had now returned to watch the fun, also had tears streaming down their faces – but of laughter.

That laughter cost many lives because the Kiowa chief, convinced that they had attempted to poison him, left the fort the following morning together with his most able warriors. They rode south with the vengeful Satanta at their head. No sooner were they out of sight of the post's garrison than, at their chief's command, they set fire to the stock of hay gathered by government contractors to help keep the many cavalry mounts and small herds of livestock fed throughout the long winter months.

'Ai-yee, this is good!' yelled Satanta as the pungent smoke from the burning hay permeated his nostrils. This, together with the cold fresh air of the fierce winter winds that scythed across the plains, seemed to cleanse his system of yesterday's poison.

'Come!' he shouted at his Kiowa followers as he kneed his mount into an all-out gallop. Exuberant at the welcome return of that freedom of movement so vital to nomadic souls everywhere, the warriors excitedly raced one another in their efforts to keep pace with their leader. The clear air was filled with their shrill laughter as they sped still further south.

At Crooked Creek Satanta, his revenge-filled mind bent on an orgy of destruction and murder aimed at all white people in his path, saw three wood cutters working industriously. He, and his two closest riders, cut the three white men down in as many seconds. The excited shouts of those warriors who arrived too late to participate in the murderous onslaught by their comrades reached a frenzied crescendo as they watched the senseless slaughter.

Only Walks-Like-A-Shadow remained silent, a troubled expression masking his normally amiable and carefree features. Satanta would have to be stopped for the good of all those Kiowas who still remained on the reservation, he told himself, but now was not the time. His beloved Summer Cloud, expecting their first child, was but one of his many relatives and friends who were hostages among white soldiers. The many would be held responsible for the few; it had ever been thus for the red peoples. It could even be that the many might be punished for the misdeeds of the few, as had been the case so often in the past. He knew all this but felt utterly powerless to change any of it. The frustration increased within him. Time was yet another enemy; for he knew that nothing other than superior force or a sudden fatal accident or illness could halt the kill-crazy chief in his present state of mind.

And so the war party continued along its road of merciless destruction. Soon it was riding through the so-called Indian Territory, still killing whites and destroying their property. After one such occasion Walks-Like-A-Shadow decided the time was as right as it ever would be to challenge Satanta's actions.

'They tried to poison me!' came the chief's snarled reply. Further attempts by the young warrior to question his leader's wisdom were curtailed even more abruptly. Satanta brushed his young follower's words aside like feathers in a wind.

But still Walks-Like-A-Shadow rode with the war chief because he alone was aware of the necessity to stop the raiding at the earliest opportunity. As much as he disliked all that he witnessed he knew that he must be where his people, all of them, most needed him.

Ironically, that loyalty to his people as he rode with Satanta throughout the bloody winter of 1869 into 1870 led to the realisation of a long held ambition for, whatever his personal feelings during those raids, his courage was undeniable. He was made a member of the elite Koh-eet-senko.

Yet Walks-Like-A-Shadow was not lifted by this honour. He was a tormented man. The Southern Plains were awash with blood and Summer Cloud was a hostage to the military. Perhaps, by now, he was a father even. But any elation occasioned by such a thought was immediately dissolved by the acid of reality for should there be a child then he or she too would be in the hands of the enemy. Icy cold fingers of fear constantly probed his mind and body as the war party continued ploughing its bloody furrow across all places occupied by whites.

# Chapter Eleven

Winter became spring which blossomed into summer which, in turn, surrendered to autumn. Still the raiding continued. The people of Texas and present day Oklahoma in particular were gripped by an intense, mind-numbing fear. Isolated ranchers, homesteaders and miners grouped together whenever circumstances permitted to form an illusion they called security.

Not only Satanta's Kiowas but also war factions from among the Comanches and other tribes of the Southern Plains were on the rampage. Killings, pillaging and arson became daily occurrences. There were breaks in the hostilities; half-hearted talks even, between warrior chiefs and white military leaders. Promises were made on both sides. Promises were broken by both sides. It was inevitable that such respites were always short-lived. Often they were merely ploys to allow one side or the other, or both, to re-equip and recuperate. Certainly the tribes needed to replenish their arms, ammunition and supplies wherever and whenever possible by whatever means necessary. And the army, stretched to its limit, even beyond at times, desperately sought rest, replacements and reinforcements.

Wiser heads, whether red or white, knew that most of the bloodshed could have been avoided if a simple wisdom had prevailed. Dismiss the corrupt officials who accumulated wealth while their evil machinations killed people daily on either side. Replace these mass-murderers with honest men who would see that Indians were fed and clothed regularly; educated but not exploited. Men who would be in positions to ensure that tribal reservation rights were not violated and that all such lands allocated to the tribes remained in their possession for their benefit and not for the making of immense profits by unscrupulous whites. But these were but pipe dreams.

Pipe dreams were of great significance and importance in the red man's culture. But to the white man pipe dreams were just puffs of smoke with no substance whatever.

Yet there was a tragic reality that the red man saw far clearer than did his white counterpart. The soldier was fighting for a weekly wage. The warrior was defending his homeland, his family, a way of life . . . he was fighting for their very existence. And so the fighting dragged on relentlessly. Autumn became winter, became spring.

Spring 1871 saw parties of surveyors criss-crossing the Indian reservation. There was talk of a railroad being constructed through it. Satanta and Satank spoke openly of war for such a project would scare all game from the Kiowa's traditional hunting grounds. And food was ever-present in their minds this spring because the expected annuities from the whites were long overdue, as usual.

The restlessness pervaded all parts of the reservation. Even those Indians who favoured peace showed signs of it. In fact, even Agent Tatum could sense it. This time he felt he had no choice other than turn to the military. He formally requested Colonel Grierson to have soldiers patrol those areas where the Kiowa fighting men normally started their forays into Texas. Grierson ordered two companies of men to cover the crossing points in an attempt to turn back any raiding parties. But one hundred soldiers, the most that he could afford to send from Fort Sill, were as so many straws placed to stop a hurricane. It was impossible! Both Grierson and Tatum were soon made aware of this. The Indian raids escalated and so did the killings. Reports of massacres and farms being abandoned poured in daily. It was not long before Texas was appealing directly to Washington.

In five years, they said, hundreds of Texans had been killed, millions of dollars worth of property had been destroyed or stolen and entire counties had been depopulated. Something had to be done. Now!

# Chapter Twelve

Satanta was cock-a-hoop! The white men were in retreat. There was no need to scalp enemies who were tearing out their own hair in fury and frustration.

Satanta was arrogant. He rode into Fort Sill in late May along with the other Kiowas coming in to collect their rations. In addition to his normal allowances he demanded that Tatum supply him with guns and ammunition for further raids into Texas. Seeing the look of bewildered disbelief on the agent's face, Satanta again displayed his fatal flaw, that deeply entrenched opinion that all white men were stupid.

He boasted to Tatum: 'You think I give you empty talk. The wagon train attacked few days ago at Salt Creek. All horses taken, all men killed, all wagons burned. I led my warriors in this victory. You do not believe? Look, I take this from one wagon driver.' He held up a large pocket watch from which a chain dangled.

The agent could not believe what was happening. Neither could Walks-Like-A-Shadow. Living up to his name, he slipped silently away from the excited Kiowas bunched around Satanta and Tatum.

Hearing the raised voices of both Satanta and Tatum, Colonel Grierson strode out from his quarters. Unabashed by the officer's sudden appearance, Satanta repeated his boast. For Grierson this was a boast too far.

He ordered the chief's immediate arrest along with two other Kiowa war leaders present, Satank and Big Tree.

Satanta shrugged off his blanket. As the blanket fell from his shoulders, Tatum and Grierson were suddenly aware of the revolver in his hand. Other warriors around him made similar threatening moves. But an order rang out clearly above the excited voices of the Kiowas. Almost at once the wooden shutters covering the windows at the front of the commanding officer's quarters flew open to reveal rows of black troopers with their carbines aimed at the Indians.

The movements and noise among the Kiowas subsided. They lowered their weapons. Those lines of levelled rifles and the grim, determined faces of the buffalo soldiers who held them unwaveringly were a risk too far; even for the Koh-eet-senko among the red fighters. Bravery was one thing. Foolishness was entirely another and not to be considered even.

Satanta, Satank and Big Tree were placed in a cell prior to being transported to Texas to face trial in the state courts there.

Yet the forays into Texas continued under the leadership of a Kiowa warrior named Lone Wolf. The frontier was still in turmoil. Violence was rampant everywhere. Very little had changed other than that more Indians remained on the reservation than previously. This time they were part of a peace faction led by Kicking Bird.

Summer Cloud was among them. Yet Walks-Like-A-Shadow continued to ride with the war faction. How else could he even hope to become an influence for peace if he could not help bring these senseless blood-drenched raids to an end. His mind was being torn apart.

As the Kiowas, Comanches and other Indians of the Southern Plains swept across the Texas border so three other Kiowas headed in the same direction but much slower and with far less enthusiasm. Satanta, Satank and Big Tree were being taken in wagons to Fort Richardson, Texas, to stand trial. All three were heavily shackled and under tight security.

Incredibly, Satank, frail and in great pain, freed himself from his chains. With raw and bloody flesh hanging from his hands and wrists where he had struggled free from his manacles this elderly, disillusioned, once great warrior started to chant the Koh-eet-senko death song. Sliding a sharp knife from beneath his blanket, he plunged it into one of the soldiers guarding him. Snatching up the wounded man's carbine, he succeeded in levering a round into its breech. But too late. Bullets from the rifles of other guards tore into his fragile frame. He died seconds later.

Satanta and Big Tree, being transported in another wagon, watched helplessly as the old warrior lost his final battle.

They were delivered to Fort Richardson and handed over to the Texans to be tried for murder. Their trial was brief. They were found guilty. Their executions were anticipated. But Governor Edmund Davis, feeling strongly that the two chiefs could exercise a restraining influence upon the Kiowas by remaining alive, commuted their sentences to life imprisonment. They were shortly bundled into a wagon and on their way to the state penitentiary; two totally dejected, desolate, devastated once-proud leaders looking forlornly out over the vast plains all around them. Their plains. Kiowa plains.

Never ending and ceilinged by an equally endless canopy of blue decorated with puff-balls of white.

Then the massive prison doors were slammed solidly shut behind them.

# Chapter Thirteen

The imprisonment of the two chiefs did nothing to curtail the incursions into Texas but it did discourage an ever-increasing number of warriors from participating in them. However, those raids which did continue were just as widespread and of an unprecedented intensity and ferocity.

The Kiowas' allies, the Comanches, saw a new young leader beginning to organise war parties against the whites. He was Quanah Parker, a half-breed, who was to write his name across history's pages as the greatest chief to emerge from the Comanche nation. His name alone began to inspire an unreasoning fear among his enemies.

But an even more dangerous factor than the Comanches in their war against the whites came in the form of the Comancheros. These were unscrupulous traders, including numerous white man, who had established their bases in the still uncharted wilderness lands of New Mexico generations earlier.

The Comancheros made a living by taking regular caravans to the Staked Plains of Texas where they traded weapons, ammunition and liquor to the Kiowas and Comanches in exchange for livestock and other pillage resulting from those Indians almost non-stop depredations.

Taken together, the ruthless Comancheros, unprincipled Indian agents and corrupt government officials proved conclusively that the biggest threat to those white inhabitants living on the south-western frontier was other whites. Their greed was a driving force that could not be stopped until the last free red man was neatly corralled with the rest of his race where the whites wanted them all to be – under their control.

Keeping a few leaders behind prison bars was having little effect to that end. Other war leaders simply sprang up to replace them.

So, with Quaker opinions being voiced loudly in places where they carried considerable sway, Satanta and Big Tree were released from the penitentiary in October 1873.

Two months later saw Lone Wolf's son and a nephew killed by cavalry in a skirmish. The old chief immediatedly embarked on a crusade of revenge. Walks-Like-A-Shadow had to make a decision; either to continue riding with Lone Wolf whose intense grief had now turned to implacable, irreversible hatred of all whites or to return to the faction headed by Satanta who, he knew, posed the biggest potential threat to Kiowa survival. He chose the latter. Whatever influence he could exert with the still powerful chief he determined to use for the benefit of the Kiowas. They must not be swept to oblivion by the white men, he told himself desperately.

Perhaps he would now be able to see his beautiful Summer Cloud again and hold their child in his arms for the first time. His longing was immeasurable.

But these were not his only thoughts as he rode to meet Satanta. Would the chief now be a force for peace? Would two years inside a white man's prison have shown him the futility of further opposition to the might of the Americans?

Within minutes of meeting Satanta, he knew the answers before even asking the questions. Prison had changed him, but not for the better. It had aged him. He now looked far older than his forty-three years. There was no longer a jovial side to his nature. He had become morose and refractory. His intense bitterness left him with but one mission in mind – revenge! He would not even speak with Walks-Like-A-Shadow.

Warriors from among all the tribes of the Southern Plains were becoming restless. The white men were still cheating them. Rations were always late and of inferior quality, often they were stale and even mouldy. Hunting became almost impossible as the once vast buffalo herds were rapidly depleted by the insatiable greed of the whites. More than one and a quarter million hides were transported by rail to eastern factories during 1872 and 1873 alone. But what could the tribes do? What should they do?

Satanta provided the catalyst. He became the terrible and terrifying driving force behind warriors from all parts of the Southern Plains. Kiowas, Comanches and even Cheyennes cut a devastating swathe of destruction and death across five states.

Late 1873 saw these areas become a blood-bath as General Sherman, with insufficient troops to defend the besieged whites, went on the offensive. He declared a state of war against the Indians.

Red and white clashed everywhere in this gargantuan struggle for the Southern Plains. Scenes of carnage were frequent and all around. There was no respite this time. The savage Red River War continued on into 1874.

Yet a third force entered into it but took no sides . . . or prisoners . . . wherever and whenever it chose to strike. The weather. On this occasion its selected site was the Southern Plains and its chosen time the summer and winter of 1874. That summer the weather relentlessly blasted the plains with a fiery heat until it became a white hot furnace and then added a drought of mind and body-sapping proportions. Whites, reds and their unfortunate mounts suffered severely. Soldiers even cut into the veins of their arms to moisten their lips with blood.

Winter was equally as remorseless with its helpless human adversaries. It tore into them with its ferocious, acutely cold northers. It teased, tormented and tortured them with every device it could. Icy winds, snow, rain, swirling blizzards, sub-zero temperatures, snow drifts, mud, frostbite; the weather pounded them persistently with every weapon in its vast armoury.

The Kiowas and their allies could not fight both the military and the weather so small numbers of warriors began to slip away and surrender at Fort Sill and other army posts. Even Quanah Parker, of the Comanches, gave up the struggle in June 1874.

Satanta finally succumbed and surrendered in October. He was a totally defeated and dejected man. He was broken. And with his surrender the heart of the Kiowa nation was broken as well. General Sherman wasted no time. He had Satanta immmediatedly re-turned to the Texas penitentiary.

Walks-Like-A-Shadow, now absolutely exhausted himself, was a man with two minds as he watched Satanta being driven away. He was almost distraught that the once supreme Satanta had been reduced to such a pathetic figure by the white men. But there was also hope within the young warrior that the thoroughly defeated Kiowas would lose no more people in a fruitless struggle against those same whites. Who could say, he asked himself. It was a question for the future to solve. He was hopeful. But he was also very, very tired.

Not long afterwards a forlorn, stooping figure, shuffled into the dispensary at Texas penitentiary and requested some medicine. 'My heart is bad,' he told the staff. He was transferred from his cell to a ward in the prison hospital. It was on the building's second storey.

Days later inmates and prison staff in the yard outside looked up as they heard a strange wailing sound coming from above them. Satanta was standing at the ward window, his arms folded against his chest. He was chanting the Koh-eet-senko death song. He took a long, sweeping look across the plains he loved and had wandered so freely. Then, a final glance at the blue skies above before plunging to his death on the stony ground beneath.

# Chapter Fourteen

Walks-Like-A-Shadow crossed and re-crossed the reservation in his desperate search for Summer Cloud and their child. He rarely stopped and then mainly to eat. He rode on relentlessly. He pushed his mount as hard as he pushed himself. But it was not until the ninth day that his spirit received a much needed boost. It took the instantly recognisable form of his friend, Short Legs.

Short Legs was standing, waiting for Walks-like-A-Shadow to reach him. This was not a time for lengthy greetings. He knew what Walks-Like-A-Shadow wanted to hear. He told him simply: 'She told several of us that if we saw you to tell you that she would be at your secret place and that you knew where that was. No more than that.'

'It is enough,' replied Walks-Like-A-Shadow who, having slowed his horse to a walking pace, now spurred it forward at a brisk gallop.

Another full day's almost non-stop hard riding brought him to that secret place. There it stood, the tepee where they had gone whenever possible to spend snatched periods of isolation, tranquility and planning during their courtship. It was much faded by the sun and recently patched in places. She was obviously still there. His heart pounded in his chest like a war drum. He had waited for this moment for so long a time.

A smile puckered the corners of his mouth as he dismounted from his horse. He crept silently across to the doorway of the tepee. He would give them a surprise.

But as he stepped inside the smile was replaced by a look of absolute horror. Summer Cloud lay spread-eagled on the ground. She was dead. So was their child, a son. The tears welled in the eyes of Walks-Like-A-Shadow. The sight of the carnage almost tore him apart. Only one thing prevented this. The boy, still so small in stature, had died a warrior's death. In his right hand he clutched a short knife, its sharp blade covered to the hilt with blood. The killer had not escaped unscathed. Now he would find that man and complete the task for his son and his beloved Summer Cloud.

His face was a mask of flint as he stepped from the tepee. Suddenly he froze, motionless. He had seen something or someone move among a rocky outcrop opposite. He waited. Less than a minute later he saw a man glide silently from those same rocks. He was moving stealthily towards Walks-Like-A-Shadow's tethered mount. The warrior felt his eyesight was betraying him. He stared in disbelief. It was the white man Quilter.

Seconds later, again showing that his name was no accident, the Kiowa stood a few yards behind Quilter. All the white man heard was the sound of a rifle hammer being eased back. He spun round. 'Good God Kiowa, you almost gave me a heart attack! What the hell you doing?'

Walks-Like-A-Shadow had anticipated a look of guilt, even anger, on Quilter's face. But not the words that had come from the white man's lips. So he did not pull the trigger. He was confused. 'You ask me this after you kill my wife and son? Are you crazy, white man?'

Now it was Quilter's turn to look nonplussed. 'Me crazy? You're the mad one. What wife? What kid? I've killed no one!'

Walks-Like-A-Shadow raised his rifle to his shoulder. 'You lie,' he said unsurely.

'I ain't lying. I came here to get me a horse. My own threw me back aways when it stepped in a pothole, busted a leg and smashed my rifle. But if you think this ain't the truth and that I killed your kin then I ain't got a chance so pull that goddam trigger and get it over with.'

A bullet struck Quilter in the right shoulder and sent him to the ground.

Walks-Like-A-Shadow looked as bewildered as did Quilter. The bullet had not come from his gun but from a point opposite. A huge Kiowa warrior, staggering drunkenly, emerged from the shadows of some trees. It was Bull Shoulders.

Quilter groaned. He was still alive, trying to staunch the flow of blood from his injured shoulder with a large kerchief. 'It's that drunken Indian. He is always around here. It was his horse I was after.'

'Don't listen,' Bull Shoulders slurred. 'He kill your woman.' As he stepped into the full sunlight he was limping. There was a knife gash in his right thigh – about as high as a small boy could reach. It was still bleeding.

In that instant Walks-Like-A-Shadow knew the truth. Bull Shoulders saw his one-time friend staring at the wound.

Both turned as one to face each other but Bull

Shoulders was slowed by his drunkeness. Walks-Like-A-Shadow's bullet hit him squarely in the chest. The massive Kiowa slumped to the ground like a falling tree trunk. Walks-Like-A-Shadow rushed over to where he fell. Bull Shoulders looked up at him. 'I took your woman. I hate you. A long time I hate you . . .' Whatever else he wanted to say remained with him as he breathed his last.

Walks-Like-A-Shadow turned as he heard a sound behind him. Quilter was attempting to struggle to his feet. The warrior ran across to help him. 'What are you trying to do white man? Kill yourself?'

'I gotta get to a doctor to stop this bleeding. Can I have his horse?' He looked in the direction of the dead Bull Shoulders.

'Where you find this doctor?'

'I know one some way from here.'

'You would never make it alone,' stated Walks-Like-A-Shadow bluntly. 'I will take you there.'

'Why?' asked Quilter. 'You don't owe me a thing Kiowa.'

'You stopped me making bad mistake. I owe you.'

Quilter was losing too much blood to argue. He nodded in dumb acceptance.

In little more than a minute the Indian had found Bull Shoulders' pony and was back at the white man's side. With some difficulty he lifted him into the saddle. Before mounting his own horse, he walked over to the tepee containing the bodies of his dead wife and child and set it ablaze. He left Bull Shoulders where he lay.

Then, astride his mount, he took the reins of the other pony, telling Quilter, 'You just hang on white man. Which way we go?' Quilter nodded towards the trail heading south. The two horses were soon moving at a steady lope.

More than three hours had passed before there was any sign of a settlement and then only a small but strongly constructed log cabin. Walks-Like-A-Shadow turned and looked at Quilter who, weak, blood-soaked but still alive, nodded back at him.

The Kiowa stopped their mounts in front of the structure's only door. Jumping to the ground, he pulled the white man carefully from his pony and rested him against the cabin wall. He banged on the door and stood back.

The door opened to reveal the twin bores of a double-barrel shotgun. It was held rock steady in the hands of a man of medium build, iron-grey hair and piercing eyes.

'What do you want?' he growled.

Walks-Like-A-Shadow indicated the reclining figure of Quilter who looked up and rasped: 'Don't point that thing at him doc. He just saved my life.'

The doctor put down the shotgun and, together with the Indian, lifted the injured man into the cabin.

Feeling uncomfortable in confined spaces, Walks-Like-A-Shadow was soon back outside and remounted. Knowing that there was nothing for him back at the reservation, he rode in the opposite direction.

As the darkness shrouded him in its cloak of total anonymity Walks-Like-A-Shadow felt his head invaded by countless thoughts of Summer Cloud, of the son he had never held and of his many dead Kiowa friends. He could no longer hold back the tears. The dam burst with a terrible ferocity.

A terrifying wail pierced the stillness. It became an almost inhuman scream of intense pain, despair and frustration at bereavements, at injustice, at the demise of his people.

Even a Koh-eet-senko had the right to cry at such a time.

# EPILOGUE

A few days after completing the book, I revisited old Shad's grave just as I had promised myself before I started writing his story. It was a long, lonely ride into the mountains but I rode lightly. In fact, the only item additional to the normal gear I carried with me on any lengthy journey, was a running iron much like those used by rustlers to alter the brands of stolen cattle.

Upon reaching the grave, I immediately built a fire and heated the running iron in it. As soon as the iron was glowing white hot I went to work on the seasoned timber which was old Shad's headboard. Once I had finished, I stood back to look at my handiwork. The fresh words I had added to the board were engraved as deeply as those that had been put there by my father originally.

SHADOW WALKER
KOH-EET-SENKO
1840?–1923
ALL-ROUND COWMAN
AND LOYAL FRIEND

Shadow Walker was simply another way of saying Walks-Like-A-Shadow. Shad had told me so. And a Kiowa who spoke fluent Spanish – a not uncommon language among the tribes of the Southwest – could pass with comparative ease as a Mexican for that race too is mainly of Indian blood. Plains Indians also often made superb cowhands having been raised on horseback almost from birth.

I cooled the running iron and replaced it in my saddle-bag. Then I carefully kicked snow over the fire until even the last few faintly glowing embers had spluttered out. As I did so, my thoughts wandered back to Shad. What would he have thought of my alterations? Inside, I knew instinctively that he would have approved and that he would have regarded my added words with pride.

Leading my horse slowly back down the mountainside, I turned round to take a last look at the grave marker of the man who had been both my friend and teacher for so many years. As I did so, I could not help but notice my ever-lengthening shadow cast dark upon the sparkling white snow by the warm red rays of the sinking sun. And as I walked I could also hear the tall pines whispering soothingly around me as their branches were stirred gently by the evening mountain breezes.

Somehow, I felt, Shadow Walker would be with me always.

# A MAN CALLED
# HUNTER

# Chapter One

'Your name sir?'

'I am called Hunter.'

The hotel desk clerk paused, pen in hand, and looked up at the man who had just requested a room. 'And your first name?' he asked.

'No other name. Just Hunter.'

'But everyone has a first name', insisted the clerk, albeit somewhat embarrased.

'No other name. Just Hunter,' repeated the man softly.

The clerk opened his mouth as if to pursue the point but was stopped by a hardness in the other man's dark brown, almost black, eyes.

'Yes sir. Just Hunter.' The clerk bent over the hotel register and entered the name. It was a relief not to have those eyes staring into his own. 'Room 11.' He took a key from a hook on a board behind him. 'Top of the stairs. End of the hall. On the left.'

'Thank you. Will you require payment in advance?' The man's voice was educated but with a slight guttural accent. His English was precise and perfect.

The clerk was visibly surprised, for although this man Hunter was attired in an immaculate dark grey suit and unblemished white shirt, he possessed high cheek-bones and skin the colour of copper. Such physical characteristics suggested more than a trace of Mexican, or even Indian, blood. His hair was black; yet short and neatly trimmed. And he was clean shaven.

The clerk recovered from his surprise. 'In advance,' he replied, somewhat uneasily. 'It's a dollar a day. Meals are extra.'

Hunter unfastened the buttons of his jacket and removed a wallet from an inner pocket. 'There. Fifty dollars. I shall be here for some time. When it is finished let me know and I will pay you further.'

'Thank you Mr Hunter,' said the clerk incredulously, for such customers were very rare in a town like Broken Leg. 'Is there anything else I can do for you?'

'Yes. I would like hot water for a bath in one hour. Then I do not wish to be disturbed for the remainder of the afternoon.'

'Yes sir.'

'And two other things. I like my room clean and my food prepared and cooked hygienically. Is that understood?'

The clerk knew the meaning of the word hygiene but had never seen it put into practice. Not in this hotel at least. However, money speaks with an eloquent tongue among greedy men so he replied: 'Certainly Mr Hunter,' making a mental note to have words with the Mexican chef and also the woman who cleaned the rooms and did the hotel laundry.

The clerk watched as hunter picked up his bags and climbed the stairs leading to his room. 'Not a big man by any means,' the clerk mused. Yet there was something about Mr Hunter, he decided, which said clearly enough that here was a man who was more than capable of looking after himself should the need arise. A man who moved with the muscular grace of a mountain lion. And those eyes . . .

'Jesus,' said the clerk quietly to himself, 'If the eyes are the mirror of the soul like they say then his ain't giving away any secrets.'

It was almost seven o'clock in the evening before Hunter came back down the stairs. He felt refreshed after his bath and subsequent sleep. Now he wanted to eat. At the reception desk the clerk, a tall, thin man who seemed all bones was talking to a small tubby Mexican who appeared to be all flesh. They looked like two stage comics he had seen in a New York theatre five years before when celebrating his twenty-first birthday. He suppressed a grin as he walked over to them and asked for a meal.

'Certainly Mr Hunter,' said the clerk. 'Beefsteak do you?'

'Very nicely thank you. But I do not like it over-cooked. Also some vegetables. I do not like them overdone either.'

'Yes sir,' nodded the clerk. 'If you would just wait in the . . . er . . . dining room.' He indicated a door at the foot of the stairs.

As Hunter entered the dining room so the tubby Mexican, who was the hotel cook, turned to the clerk. 'What ees all thees "yes sir" for? He don' look a very important man. He looks very much like one of my peoples to me. And I never before hear you say "yes sir" to a Mexican. Also, what ees thees dining room? We don' have no dining room.'

'When a man pays the kind of money that Mr Hunter pays I'll call a room any goddam name I think he wants it called. And, another thing, he may look like a Mex but he sure enough doesn't speak like one. Probably from that there Europe across the Atlantic,' he added with the air of a man who possesses knowledge superior to that of the people around him.

'But he ees not white whatever you say mi amigo,' insisted the little Mexican who was called Pedro by everyone in town because nobody could pronounce his correct name due to its unbelievable length and complexity.

His tall, angular colleague refused to give ground. 'They ain't all white over there. Not in Spain. Nor Italy. I seen it in books. Or he may even be one of them rich Arab chiefs. But, whatever he is, it ain't Mexican and you'd better get into the kitchen and cook what he asked for.'

The cook waddled towards the kitchen muttering to himself in Spanish. As an afterthought the clerk added, 'And don't forget to wash your hands first. Or the food before you cook it.' So saying he walked into the dining room. It was a small room containing three circular wooden tables with four chairs to each.

He went across to the table at which Hunter had seated himself. From his position Hunter was able to see both the door and also the window which overlooked the town's main street. The clerk did not notice such things. Wherever money was not involved he was never a very observant man. 'Your meal will not be long Mr Hunter,' he said.

'I am in no hurry. All I intend to do this evening is to get to know your town a little better. Do you know it very well?'

'Been here since it started. Must have been about thirteen, nearly fourteen, years back,' returned the clerk, somewhat proudly.

148

'Is that so Mr . . .'

'Wooller, James Wooller.'

'Well, Mr Wooller, then you must know Mr Charles Buckner.'

'Yes sir Mr Hunter. Everybody in Broken Leg knows Mr Buckner. Hell, he is Broken Leg. Even gave the town its name. Was on his way west about fourteen years ago to start a business in California when he took some kind of a tumble from his horse which ran off straight after. He couldn't chase it 'cause he had a busted leg.

'Dead lucky though. Someone came along right off while he was trying to fix his leg with a couple of make-shift splints. And damned if the feller that found him wasn't some kind of travelling salesman with a wagon full of goods. Mr Buckner had a wad of money on him and bought him out, lock, stock an' barrel. He had been travelling along a regular route when his horse throwed him so he just set up business right there. The town kind of grew round him. I was one of the very first. You a friend of his Mr Hunter?'

'Not exactly. But my father and a number of relatives helped start him in business, in a manner of speaking. Before you knew him of course.'

'Then he'd be right pleased to see you I guess.'

'No. I doubt that. We only met once and that was very briefly. I was a small boy and I am sure he would never recognise me now. However, it pays to become better acquainted with the influential citizens of any township do you not agree?'

'Yes sir. No doubt about that.'

'Therefore, I intend to become better acquainted with Mr Buckner. I feel that it will do me much good in the end.'

At this point the conversation was interrupted by the arrival of Hunter's meal. Pedro had excelled himself and the clerk found the saliva forming in his own mouth as Hunter started to cut into the thick, succulent steak surrounded by a variety of vegetables.

'Will that be all Mr Hunter?' he asked as he prepared to leave the dining room.

Hunter looked up. 'Yes. Thank you Mr Wooller.' Then, added as an afterthought, 'Unless you can tell me where Mr Buckner would normally be found at this time of the day.'

'Well, usually he'd be at the saloon across the street. The Palace. He owns it. But you won't find him there tonight. He's away, on business.'

Hunter raised his head slightly and lowered his fork with a large chunk of meat still skewered to it. 'What a pity. Is he often away on business?'

Always eager to display his knowledge of Broken Leg's current affairs the clerk replied: 'Quite often Mr Hunter. Sometimes there's quite a space between trips. But still quite often.'

'Thank you Mr Wooller. One further favour please.'

'Yes sir. You just name it.'

'I do not wish anyone to know of this conversation between us until I have seen Mr Buckner personally. Not even Mr Buckner himself. Do you understand?'

'Of course Mr Hunter. I won't mention it to anyone.'

'That is good,' then, judging the clerk to be a man more easily swayed by money than threats, he gave him a ten dollar note.

'Thank you Mr Hunter sir. Any time you want any other favours just ask. Yes sir. Just ask.'

# Chapter Two

Hunter walked leisurely from the comparative quiet of the hotel into the night life of Broken Leg. It was much like other border towns he had ridden through. Three saloons were going full blast. Americans and Mexicans mingled and jostled in numbers which were more or less even. The inequality of Broken Leg, as with many other similar townships, rested not with its racial statistics but with the degrees of good and bad. Hunter sighed. Why did the disreputable element of such settlements always outweigh the decent?

He strolled casually along the main street. He appeared completely at ease but his eyes never remained still for longer than a few seconds. They were probing continually the darkness around him. The town was honeycombed with alleys among the many buildings of various heights which were Broken Leg. If a shadow floated across any of the pools of light pouring from the windows and doorways around him then he saw it. He missed nothing.

A couple of drunks staggered from one bar and lurched across the road to another saloon which stood almost opposite. Hunter stopped and remained as still as a wooden post. Neither of them saw him standing in the shadows, yet he absorbed everything they wore, said and did. As they entered the saloon so Hunter started walking again. He grinned to himself. Old habits die hard, he thought. Still, it was good to keep in practice for if such habits ever did die in him then so would he die soon after.

Two men out on a drunken spree. Nothing wrong in that. One American, the other Mexican. Nothing wrong in that either. Good for racial harmony, he told himself cynically. But both wearing guns. Why did the people of such border towns always carry guns? Were they not aware that the last frontiers had been crossed and the West finally 'civilised'. Good God it was almost six years since the last of the so-called Indian uprisings, had been crushed. That was the Ghost Dance craze of December 1890 when so many Sioux people had been needlessly and wantonly slaughtered at Wounded Knee Creek.

So why the guns? Why the town? Situated in the middle of the arid south-west corner of New Mexico, it was a mere two or three miles from the Mexican border. There were no ranches or mines around it. The only possible reason for its existence would have to be trade. And guns always meant trouble, particularly when they were worn by the dubious types he had seen wearing them. Humanity was much like a cup of really good coffee. A little cream, a large amount of strong, decent liquid refreshment and, finally, no matter how good the coffee, the dregs. Bitter dregs which were always thrown out because no one could stomach them. Broken Leg was mainly dregs. It would make a rotten cup of coffee, Hunter smiled wryly to himself.

What kind of trade? All things on the surface. But underneath? Running guns across the border into Mexico? Probably. There was always a ready market there. Revolutionaries against the country's dictatorial and ruthless president, Porfirio Diaz. Bandits. And sometimes an indistinguishable mixture of both.

Hunter's leisurely walk had now taken him past the outskirts of the town into the cool, fresh, cloudless atmosphere of the desert at night. It was like coming home, he thought. He always felt at home in the desert. The desert, like the sea, was forever capable of placing man in his correct perspective. A microscopic particle of dust within the eternity of the universe. No sooner placed under the microscope than blown away, never to be seen again. The desert was a good place for a man to think and, for many, a place of fear also.

Hunter looked back at Broken Leg, bathed in the light of an almost full moon. It too was placed in its correct perspective, when viewed at a distance, by the emptiness surrounding it. A sprawling mess of adobe or wooden blocks that looked as if they had been scattered haphazardly across the landscape from some gigantic dice-shaker.

Some learned people compared the desert to the surface of the moon, saying that there was a great similarity. He, like such people, had also viewed the moon through a powerful telescope. And they were wrong. Perhaps other deserts of the world bore some resemblance to the moon's surface but not this one. The moon was dead. but not this desert; his desert. It was alive. The pulse was erratic at times but its beat was always incredibly strong. And on nights like this, he thought, you could almost feel it.

Hunter looked around him at the beauty of the desert by night and breathed its fragrance deep into his lungs. He could never have enough of the desert. To most it represented an enormous void with death ever present in a hundred different guises. And for the majority of people death was indeed the sole host of this vast wilderness.

For Hunter, however, the situation was the exact reverse. The desert literally breathed life into him. It swept away the depressions that sometimes affected his mood among people in towns and large settlements. Not that he was a hermit. No, far from that. It was more a disenchantment with humanity that other people instilled in him occasionally. So many of them were forever grasping for more than they needed. Much more. And in such devious ways.

He strode further from the town, still sucking the clear night air deep down inside his lungs. Even in its violence, as with the infrequent cloudbursts and consequent flash floods, the desert had none of the complexities that were the human mind. Small wonder the Indians had fought so long and hard to keep it. And yet their ways were much like their environs; even their violence had an honesty about it that could never hope to match the countless deceitful ploys of their white enemies.

That was why all of them had been conquered in turn. The Zunis, Hopis, Pueblos, Navajos and finally, a decade ago after fifty years of terrible warfare, the Apaches.

He smiled bitterly. The American government had fought for so long for so large a region and yet still occupied only a handful of small areas which were merely a sparse scattering of pinpricks on any map of the Southwest. Was it purely aggression on the part of the United States? Or was it more a desire to acquire by any means whatever as much territory as possible? After all, was not greed one of man's most powerful driving forces.

A sparse scattering of pinpricks. When would the Americans learn that it was impossible to fight the desert and win? It had never lost a battle. The Indians, particularly the Apaches, had learned this lesson centuries before. The desert was a good friend to those who adapted to its ways and allowed them to live off it accordingly. But to those unable to readjust to its relentless pressures it was a ruthless enemy and crushed them remorselessly.

Hunter knew how to live in the desert. That was why he was here. That and the possibility that Broken Leg was the source of gun-running across the border into Mexico.

President Diaz had become more than a little concerned about the recent increase in the illegal import of United States arms and ammunition into his country. There were rumblings in many parts of Mexico and he was worried. Bandits were one thing but revolutionaries were another. And revolutionaries armed with modern American weapons were something else yet again. He wanted it stopped immediately so he had had a discreet word in the American ambassador's ear who, in turn, had contacted his government in Washington.

Hunter, a United States marshall, had been hand-picked for the assignment. His chief in Washington had told him: 'You know the border area like the back of your hand. Sometimes I'd swear you're as Indian as you look if I didn't know better. You're the most intelligent and educated of my staff in the field. And you like working solo. This last thing is important because a group of my boys working together might scare them off.

'And I don't want that. I want this gun-running stopped. You know why I want it stopped? Because the

President of the United States wants it stopped. And he does my thinking for me on this score. Officially, you've got to stick to the book and use only legal methods to stop it. But you know me and, even better, I know you Hunter. You use any damn means you have to, unofficially of course, to put these boys out of business. Not just temporarily either. For good. Be your usual smooth, underhanded, conniving self and I'll be more than happy. But stop these bastards before we find ourselves with a border war on our hands.'

During the following months of investigation all roads led to one town and one man. Broken Leg and Mr Charles Buckner.

The leisurely stroll into the desert became a nightly routine for Hunter. Knowing your possible quarry was one thing. Obtaining sufficient proof, however, to nail his hide to the barn door was another thing completely. So Hunter walked and waited.

On the fifth evening after his arrival at Broken Leg his walking and waiting were rewarded.

As on the four previous occasions he was south of the town. Yet this time there was a difference. Tonight he was unable to hear the usual nocturnal sounds of the desert wildlife. These nightly noises were stilled. Something had disturbed the animals, birds and reptiles which made them. And that something was the scuffing of muffled hooves against the sand and rock over which they moved. Hunter's trained ears were immediately able to identify the animals concerned. Mules. Mules pulling wagons, also with the wheels muffled in some way. Empty wagons for they were bouncing somewhat as they rolled along.

The sounds came from somewhere to his right and

they were coming from the direction of the Mexican border. As swiftly and silently as an Apache on the trail of an enemy he ghosted across the area separating him from the route the mules were following.

Concealed by the shadow of a towering saguaro cactus he was able to watch them closely as they passed by in the light of what was now a full moon. Three open box-type wagons with the wheels bound all around with heavy duty sacking. Each vehicle drawn by a team of four mules in pairs. The hooves of these animals were covered by specially made shoes of hide; each one pulled together at the top to prevent it slipping off. And two men to a wagon.

Scruffy but capable looking, they all had the appearance of men who enjoyed a fight and would not ride around one if the choice was theirs. However, if he was correct in his assumptions and they had just returned from a gun-running jaunt south of the border then the choice was not theirs but that of whoever paid them. Hence the muffled hooves and wheels.

More sounds. A bunch of horses being ridden steadily. Their hooves were not covered and made more noise than the small cavalcade which had just passed him. Pursuit? No. If this had been the case then the teamsters ahead would have heard them also and made a move of some kind. They were, however, completely unruffled.

The horses and their riders, eight in all, jogged past Hunter. Less than two yards separated him from their path but he remained as motionless as the cactus itself and they failed to see him. He smiled inwardly. His superior in Washington was right. Few people could use the desert as Hunter could use it. Not even these obviously experienced nightriders.

Fourteen men. A small army and extremely well-armed. This was going to be a tough assignment beyond doubt. Yet he was curiously satisfied with it for he had recognised Buckner as one of the horsemen. And Hunter was eager to settle a long outstanding account with this man. The odds were against the debt ever being collected but Hunter had one great advantage over his adversary. For, although they had met previously, Buckner would never recognise him because Hunter had been only ten years old at the time whereas Buckner, now into middle age, had changed very little.

Hunter followed his quarry as silently as the giant cats which stalked the high mountains to the west. And, just like those same animals, he remained unseen by the prey he pursued. There was an expression of fierce joy on his face which betrayed the exhilaration he always experienced on such occasions. Some men needed the stimulus of alcohol to produce such a feeling within themselves but not this man. He was as much a hunter by instinct as by name. A curious coincidence but an apt one, he reflected.

The riders ahead of him were making for a cluster of wooden buildings and corrals about half a mile the Mexican side of Broken Leg. He moved in closer and watched as the mules were led into what appeared to be a large barn, unharnessed from the wagons and then brought out again to feed from the troughs which lined one of the fences which penned them in. The six men who had been with the wagons quickly saddled and mounted horses from an adjacent corral. Then all fourteen riders galloped towards the town, laughing and shouting as they rode.

Hunter did not follow them. Instead he glided stealthily across to the large wooden structure which housed the wagons. He moved cautiously because of the possibility of one or more guards being left on duty to watch the property. Although he had seen no evidence of this, he still used all his skills when approaching the huge shed. A man without caution in his business was soon without breath as well. Never underestimate your enemy. Never employ your talents to less than capacity in any situation where even the slightest danger existed.

A swift yet silent and thorough search of the building revealed no guards. Hunter walked over to the three wagons he had watched being brought in. He climbed into one of them. Deep scratches in the bottom and along the lower sides indicated a heavy load. Splinters of wood of a different type to that of the wagon itself meant that the goods had been conveyed in wooden crates. And small pieces of sacking snagged at various intervals along the top edges of the wagon box, together with a scattering of grain across the wagon floor, were clear evidence that sacks of grain had been placed on top of the heavier merchandise in order to conceal it from any casual observer. The guards who rode with the wagons were obviously an insurance against the remote possibility of a closer inspection and the night was also a close ally when it came to concealment.

Leaping down from the wagon Hunter proceeded to search the other two with equal diligence. The second produced sound reason for speculation that these vehicles had indeed been used for running guns and ammunition across the border. Much larger splinters of wood showed where a crate had broken open along one of its edges. And the numerous dull grey marks along the inside of the wagon at this same point revealed that it had been rubbed continuously for some time by pieces of lead. Or, if Hunter was correct, by the noses of bullets as they were jolted up and down for a considerable distance.

# Chapter Three

As he walked slowly back to town Hunter considered how the problem should be tackled. There was really only one answer. It had to be done from the inside. A solitary operator could accomplish nothing from the outside; that much was evident. How to get inside? With so little time at his disposal Hunter decided on a blunt approach. Buckner was nobody's fool but that could be an advantage. Who would expect a man as educated as Hunter obviously was to be anything less than devious if he was a government agent? Certainly no intelligent man he had ever encountered. Grinning slightly to himself he strode along the main street and in through the doors of the Palace Saloon. He would ask Buckner for employment.

Hunter threaded his way through the packed room and waited patiently while those ahead of him were served by the bar tender. Then came his turn. 'Brandy please.' He had acquired a taste for quality liquor during his time in the East and had no stomach for the raw alcohol of the frontier. Rotgut was, in his opinion, a most accurate description as well as appropriate term, for the so-called whisky of such establishments as this.

A hand pushed him roughly aside. 'Whisky!' roared the man responsible. 'You can serve this milksop after you've served the men first. And he ain't no man. Are you sonny?'

He turned to face Hunter who had recovered his balance and now stood less than a yard away. At that distance it was impossible to miss the rancid odour of the man's breath. If he was not yet drunk, thought Hunter, then he was only a drink or so away from being just that. 'Anything you say old timer,' smiled Hunter pleasantly.

'Are you trying to make an ass out of me?' The man was heavily bearded but he was no old timer. Perhaps in his late thirties or early forties.

'There's no sense in my attempting to do what nature has already accomplished so admirably.' The smile was still there but only a fool would have missed the danger behind it. And most men he had met were basically fools, reflected Hunter as he watched the other's face slowly turn colour until it was deep red with anger. They saw only what they wanted to see; the consequences of which had proved disastrous to all those who had seen this immaculately attired, slightly built man as a soft dandy. A perceptive man would not have been so stupid. He would have read the truth in Hunter's eyes just as the hotel clerk had done.

The bearded man was perhaps four inches taller than Hunter and outweighed him by at least sixty or seventy pounds. He turned to those around him, many of whom looked as if they had been cast from the same mould. 'Did you hear that?' Now, wouldn't you say this milksop's outgrowed his britches?'

They all laughed and several nodded in agreement. 'What you going to do about it Jackson?' asked one.

Jackson tugged at his beard as if in deep meditation. 'Well boys I been thinking . . .'

'Impossible,' interrupted Hunter lightly. Make the

man really lose his temper and he would be far easier to handle.

'Sonovabitch!' The bearded man reached out to grab Hunter but his opponent was no longer there. He was to Jackson's left side stinging the bigger man across the cheek with an open hand. The man gasped, in amazement rather than pain, turned and lunged again. For a second time he missed his quarry who had leaped lightly away. 'Stand still you blasted fairy!' he bellowed.

'Anything to oblige,' replied Hunter, doing exactly as requested.

Sensing trickery Jackson made no move to grab him this time. Instead he suddenly lashed out a heavily booted foot. With a grace and swiftness which were almost unbelievable to those present, Hunter arched backwards to avoid the kick; at the same time cupping his hands behind the heel of the boot and levering upwards. Jackson fell backwards and struck the floorboards of the saloon with such force that bottles and glasses rattled against the bar on which they rested.

Some of the men stopped laughing. Even the piano ceased its perpetual jangle as the man who played it left his seat to watch the fun. For in his humble opinion anything that caused pain to Jackson fell into that category. He, himself, had suffered constant humiliation at the hands of this drunken bully.

Suddenly, the crowd started laughing again. But this time at Jackson and not with him. The big man pushed himself to his feet. 'I'll deal with this little sod first. Then I'll continue the argument with anyone else who still feels like laughing.'

Some of the laughter stopped but not all of it. One raucous voice shouted encouragingly: 'Come on dude.

Sort the fat slob out. Try some more fancy tricks on him.'

A man used always to winning and without any finesse whatsoever, Jackson simply lowered his head like an enraged bull and charged his opponent. Hunter stepped nimbly to one side and employed the other's impetus and weight to end the fight in one movement. Using Jackson's outstretched left arm as a lever Hunter pivotted neatly, arched his back and hurled the huge man several yards. Jackson's back struck the edge of a table, breaking two of its legs in the process. He tried to raise himself from the wreckage but slumped to the floor, groaning and barely semi-conscious.

'My God, how the hell did you do that?' asked the piano-player, now standing beside Hunter.

'It's called ju-jitsu,' answered Hunter calmly. 'An ancient form of wrestling originated by the Japanese. It is the art of using your opponent's speed and weight to your own advantage by employing a variety of leverage throws. It has some useful holds as well which, if applied correctly, can render a man or,' he grinned, 'should you prefer, a woman quite helpless.'

Those who heard these last words laughed uproariously. One of them picked up Hunter's low-crowned, narrow-rimmed black stetson which had fallen off during the brief tussle. 'Here you are dude, I mean mister.'

Hunter replaced his hat securely on his head. The remainder of his clothing was as unruffled and immaculate as when he first entered the saloon. He turned to the barman. 'Is my brandy ready please?'

'Just coming up sir. It'll only take a . . . Look out!' he roared, pointing behind Hunter.

Jackson had regained consciousness and staggered to

his feet. He was starting to pull his revolver from its holster as the bar tender yelled his warning.

Hunter pirouetted as neatly and swiftly as a ballet dancer. During that same movement he had smoothly taken his own handgun from its waxed leather holster below his left shoulder in an incredibly fast cross-draw. Stooping into a slight crouch, legs apart and bent at the knees, he squeezed the trigger twice, his right wrist steadied by gripping it with his left hand. Either shot would have killed the bearded bully. They were both in his heart, a little more than an inch separating the two bullets. At a nod from the barman two men dragged the body outside.

Hunter looked around warily but, seeing no further signs of trouble, slid the revolver back into its holster. A small pistol and a small holster. When his jacket was hanging correctly, as it was now, neither was noticeable. The gun was the new Colt .32 which had been in production since only the previous year, 1895. Popularly know as the 'Police Special' it was used also by people who worked outside the law, particularly in the East. Here in the Southwest, however, men still favoured the larger handguns. The Colts .44 and .45 and a number of other revolvers of similar size and calibre were those seen most commonly.

While the men about him were still discussing excitedly the shooting they had just witnessed, Hunter calmly reminded the barman: 'My brandy please. Third time lucky I hope.'

'Third time lucky?' echoed the bar tender.

'Certainly. Is this not the third time I have ordered a glass of brandy?' And on the previous two occasions have I not been interrupted without you even reaching the point of pouring? So third time lucky. That is if no one else attempts to disturb us again.'

'No chance. I've seen some fast draws in this place. And so have they. But no one ever come near your speed. They ain't going to try. They seen you fight. With your hands and with your gun. They'll leave you alone if it means facing you on even terms.'

'But what about when things are not even? When it is dark or when my back is turned?'

'All border towns are rough. I should know. I've been in enough of them. This here's no better than most; worse perhaps. I like the money so I stay strictly neutral. Now, whatever you are mister, you ain't neutral. I mean, Jackson was a loud-mouthed son-of-a-bitch but even he had friends. So you got enemies. No, mister, you'd better look out for your back, specially in the dark.' He finished pouring Hunter's brandy, gave it to him and moved on to serve another customer.

'I overheard what the barman was telling you,' said a voice to hunter's left. Hunter turned. It was Buckner. 'And he's right my friend. You'd better not stay in Broken Leg too long.'

Buckner had altered little since the first time Hunter had seen him sixteen years previously. Well over six feet tall he was built like a prizefighter. His thick dark brown hair, which just reached his collar, now had streaks of grey in it. His face was somewhat fatter and his waistline a trifle thicker. But these were the only changes. The ruthlessness and cunning were still in his eyes for any perceptive man to see. He appeared smooth enough on the surface yet underneath this silky facade nothing had changed. In his kind it never did.

Hunter betrayed none of the hatred he had held for

this man for so long. 'Thank you for the friendly warning. However, I intend staying for a while. A considerable while in fact.'

'Then the only chance you got of staying alive is to work for me. I've got a helluva lot of influence in this town and I could use a man with your talents son.'

'While thanking you for the offer I am afraid I must decline it. I came to Broken Leg to work for a Mr Charles Buckner.'

'Well you're talking to him right now. I'm Charlie Buckner. And I don't know you boy.'

Hunter turned and held out his hand but withdrew it when the other man made no move. 'Glad to know you Mr Buckner. You wouldn't know me. But you knew my father. He was involved in a business deal concerning you and some friends fifteen or sixteen years ago.'

Buckner's eyes narrowed. 'I never knew anyone in those days with your kind of education. What was your pa's name?'

'Hunter. The same as mine. But he was not educated in the manner I am. However, selling Apache Indian scalps in bulk would raise sufficient money to buy a very good education would you not agree?'

Buckner relaxed a little. 'Yeah, I guess it would but I don't remember anybody called Hunter.'

'Do you remember the names of all those who rode with you on that occasion?'

'Hell no boy. They were such a mixed bunch. Whites, Mexicans, breeds. Even a nigger. So your pa told you all about our little scalp hunt? Man, that was really something. You never saw anything like it in your whole damn life. The braves were all away hunting or something. Just old men, women and children left behind in the village. It was so blasted easy. Just like a turkey shoot.

'Except for one big crippled buck. Used to be a chief someone said. Cazador they called him. He put up a helluva scrap. Killed him myself. And all his family. What a harvest! The Mexican government paid us handsomely for those scalps. A hundred American dollars for each one. A small fortune. My share started me in business. Now I own nearly all this goddam town.

'That's why I could use a man like you. Like an extra right arm. You can't grow big without making enemies, specially in a place like this. I got a finger in every pie. I'd pay you well. Real well, I mean.'

'That would be just fine Mr Buckner.'

'Just one thing puzzles me though. How come with your education you're willing to work as a bodyguard for me? And why come looking for me in the first place? Answers sonny. The right ones and the job's yours.'

Hunter was calm. 'Education does not automatically bring wealth,' he replied, staring hard-eyed at the big man. 'And I like the good life. My father is dead now so, before what money I had ran out, I started thinking deeply and moving around a great deal.

'During my travels your name came up in a conversation and I remembered it from my father's days. Someone said you were making a fortune down here. So I came looking for you; hoping that should you see fit to employ me then I could learn from you and, in so doing, ease a little of that wealth my way.'

Buckner laughed. 'Fair enough. Fair enough.' He was flattered. 'You'll learn plenty; that's for damn sure. And the pickings that come your way will have a lot of meat on them and you'll grow fat on them. That's equally for damn sure. So let's drink to it. Easy pickings and good living.' He tossed back the whisky he was holding and Hunter drained his brandy glass.

# Chapter Four

Hunter became Broken Leg's first-ever sheriff, appointed by Buckner. The town was like a storehouse of kegs containing gunpowder mixed with nails. Unstable kegs which often exploded. Whenever one did it was Hunter's task to ensure that none of the nails flew in his employer's direction. He did an excellent job. Wherever Buckner went he went; always slightly behind the bigger man like some small dark shadow. People laughed at their new sheriff. But never loudly enough for him, or the man who hired him, to hear them. Some wag christened Hunter 'Buckner's tail'. The name stuck. But, again, they never said it loudly enough for either man to hear. Both men knew of course. But as long as they never actually heard anyone say it they did not let it bother them.

The new sheriff was small, dark and forever just to the rear of Buckner. Any resemblance to a shadow, however, ended there. For no shadow could be as fast or as deadly as this man called Hunter. If he was 'Buckner's tail' then that tail had a sting in it like no other.

Like so many other frontier towns before and after it, Broken Leg's reputation of being 'wide-open' attracted more than its fair share of undesirables. Many of them were homicidal psychopaths. No one was as fast or as accurate with a gun as they were. Authority was for others, not for them. The only law they acknowledged was the law of violence. The people who accepted authority dealt with Buckner. Those who did not dealt with Hunter. The people in the first of these two categories were infinitely better off.

One after another, those men who went against Buckner's authority found themselves facing Hunter. And, one after another, they succumbed to either his 'Jap wrestling', as the townspeople called it, or his gun.

Buckner found himself more powerful than at any other time in his life. He enjoyed the feeling. He came to rely on Hunter more and more. The big man confided in his bodyguard. Many of Buckner's decisions were the result of conferring with Hunter's educated mind. And Hunter encouraged such trends in Buckner. It was only a matter of time before Buckner would find his 'tail' indispensable. When that time arrived he would have forgotten that a scorpion was capable of stinging itself to death with its own tail. Hunter was content to wait.

As the weeks went by so the two men screwed the lid down as tightly as possible on the town without actually discouraging people from letting off steam in Broken Leg and spending their money there. The border ruffians continued to consider the town 'wide-open' but the two men knew better. Buckner continued to smile and Hunter continued to wait.

For the first time in months Hunter found himself with time to relax. He no longer needed to be continually in his employer's company. Buckner was safe enough without Hunter actually being with him. His bodyguard's reputation was sufficient. The thought of retribution in the form of this slightly built man with the speed and deadliness of a rattlesnake deterred even the

171

toughest of the town's rougher element from going against Buckner.

What to do with his leisure time? That was never any problem for Hunter when he was in this part of the country. The desert. Unlike those entertainments concocted by man himself which were in one place today and in another tomorrow, the desert was always there. And, unlike those diversions of man which have become institutions in towns throughout the world, the desert never presented the same face twice.

It was forever changing. The sun, wind and rain ensured that this process of continual alteration would never stop. The sun dried and cracked the earth and the rocks. The wind blew the resultant fragments in all directions. Then the brief but violent storms would bring flash floods which could move countless tons of earth and rock in such a short interval of time that the result was practically inconceivable. This erosion by the sun, wind and rain would go on forever, Hunter told himself. It would continue long after man who, like the entertainments he devised, was here today and gone tomorrow. There had been an earth before mankind arrived. There would still be an earth after he departed.

But there was much more to the desert than the slow processes of erosion. The sun, when it arose each morning and set every evening, gave the land a tremendous variety of incredible colours that no artist could ever match with his brush and palette. The wind carved a multitude of intricate patterns across the landscape, the magnitude of which no sculptor could recreate. And the rain gave it life. The comparatively long life of certain species of tree and cactus; the shorter life of the desert's unique animals, reptiles and birds; the brief yet spectacular life of the many varied blooms which decorated the plant forms following a heavy rainfall. Such things gave the desert a breathing and, at the same time, breathless beauty.

Hunter knew all this and loved it. Yet there was always something more to learn. So most of his leisure time was spent riding, and sometimes walking, across many parts of the desert country around Broken Leg.

Never seen unless he wanted it so he would frequently pit himself against the land in an effort to increase his endurance, the speed of his reflexes, his physical fitness, the power of his thinking and the acuteness of his senses.

To achieve such objectives he ran great distances without stopping for rest, climbed difficult rock faces, hunted animals on foot, killed snakes with just a knife and shot birds while they were still in flight.

Such things were also challenges. And Hunter thrived on challenges as a vampire bat does on flesh blood. They were the very essence of his being. Perhaps it was as much the challenge of tracking and catching a lawbreaker as Hunter's sense of justice that made him such a superb lawman. Unorthodox, perhaps, yet undeniably the best in his particular field of action in the employ of the United States government.

Shooting was not just a method of sharpening his reflexes either. He spent long hours at it, striving for maximum efficiency, accuracy and speed. His weapons were always in excellent working order. He would check and clean them thoroughly after every practice session.

For close solo combat when an opponent was armed and there was no opportunity to disarm him Hunter would use either his Colt .32 or his knife, a leather-handled eight inch slither of the finest steel honed to razor sharpness along both edges. In order to break up an attacking force of several men at close quarters he had chosen a Parker 10-gauge shotgun with both barrels sawn down to barely twelve inches in length. It was a superb weapon and extremely effective at short range.

But his favourite gun was the rifle he used for distance work. It was a lever-action 1895 model Savage .303 with a twenty-six inch barrel and a six-shot rotary type magazine. Fully loaded it weighed only a little over seven pounds. The barrel had been dulled to a blue-grey non-smooth finish to prevent it reflecting any glare from the sun or other light sources. To Hunter the rifle was a work of art, custom-made for him alone just as a master violinist has his own instrument made especially for him only to play. And just as the master violinist could play his own instrument as no one else could, so Hunter had developed an incredible skill with his .303 Savage. Had anyone seen him use it they would have found it practically impossible to give credence to what they saw. But he always worked alone and no man at whom he fired ever got sufficiently close to watch him at work.

No one had ever devised better footwear for use in the desert than the Apache Indians. Hunter always carried a pair of their calf-length moccasins in his saddle bags when he rode out of town. He wore them whenever running, climbing or tracking. Few animals heard him approach. No human being ever did.

Having left his horse tied in a small concealed arroyo, Hunter was inching his way up a particularly difficult rock climb when he first heard the shots. Rifle fire. Approximately a mile to his north-east.

He returned rapidly to the base of the rock face. Without changing back into his clothes and boots which were packed neatly in his saddlebags, he leaped onto his mount, a light brown mustang with both speed and endurance.

Urging his horse swiftly over the boulder-strewn ground separating him from the area of gunfire he looked more like a wild Indian than a United States marshal. He was still wearing the almost knee-length moccasins into which were tucked the legs of a soiled pair of jeans he always wore when climbing, running or hunting in the desert. His bare chest, back and arms, brown and glistening with sweat in the hot sun, did nothing to dispel this appearance. Only his short and neatly trimmed hair would have caused doubt in an onlooker's mind.

But Hunter had no intention of being seen. He guided the mustang with superb horsemanship across land that offered adequate concealment to those who knew it well. His keen eyesight, coupled with the clarity of the desert air, soon picked out minute puffs of smoke as the rifles continued their firing. However, his acute sense of hearing was now able to divide the shooting into three distinct groups. He continued riding hard. At this distance and with all the noise around them neither the attackers nor the attacked would hear him he knew.

At a distance of a little more than five hundred yards from the scene he could see everything clearly. He halted his horse and dismounted. Leaving it behind a rocky upthrust he drew his Savage .303 rifle from its scabbard along the right hand side of his saddle. Checking to see that it was fully loaded and taking an extra box of cartridges with him, he sprinted over to a small group of boulders which gave him a commanding view of the entire situation.

There were three areas of firing, he confirmed. Two pairs of riflemen, one pair on either side of a steep-walled canyon, were firing down onto the stagecoach which made a weekly run into Broken Leg. With its two lead mules put out of action by shots from above, the coach could not move but the driver and guard had managed to scramble beneath the vehicle and return the fire of their attackers. A long-barrelled handgun was being used with some accuracy from inside the coach as well.

The men above were not having it all their own way for fragments of flying rock caused by the marksmanship of those below caused them to duck frequently. But it was obviously only a matter of time before the defenders of the coach succumbed. Their position was virtually untenable for any considerable period from the concentrated fire pouring down on them.

Hunter eased himself into a comfortable firing position. From the pocket of his jeans, where he had placed it before climbing from his mount, he drew a slender, short but powerful telescope and clipped it onto his rifle just to the front of the hindsight. A simple adjustment and he was able to see the bandits as distinctly as if they were but a street's width distant.

Knowing that the two on the far side of the canyon would be the most difficult to bring down once they were aware of his presence he centred aim in that direction first. Two rapid shots, with only a slight sideways movement of his rifle in between them, and both men were down.

Swinging the Savage's barrel to cover the near side of the canyon, he peered through the telescopic sight. The remaining two attackers had ceased firing and were looking around anxiously to see where the new offensive against them was coming from. Hunter gave them no chance. Aiming carefully at each in turn, he shot them both as he would have a couple of rabid dogs. And with fewer qualms. For, in any final analysis, the disease-stricken dogs would not have known any better.

Pausing only to ensure that there were no others involved in the attack on the coach he changed back into his normal immaculate attire and headed for town at a gallop. He had no desire to be seen by any of the people he had rescued for at this point he had no way of know-ing whether the bandits had been in Buckner's employ or not. If they had been, and he had allowed himself to be seen by the people from the coach, then he knew he would have been in Buckner's bad books for a long, long time. Too long for him to do the task he had set out to accomplish. Besides, as sheriff he had no jurisdiction outside the town limits and he was in no position to reveal his status of United States marshal.

## Chapter Five

He had been back in Broken Leg for longer than three hours and was lazing on his bed in the hotel when the coach arrived. The window was open and he heard clearly the excitement of the people outside. Words floated through the lace curtains and into the room as if carried on a current of air.

A booming voice, obviously belonging to the coach driver, almost shouted: 'You should've been there. The bastards, four of 'em we counted, had shot my two lead mules down and were all set to do the same to us. Me and Johnny was pinned under the coach with this lady and gent inside.' The word 'lady' caused Hunter to turn his head slightly and listen with more interest to what the booming voice was saying.

'The lady was as brave as she is pretty, if you don't mind me saying so ma'am.' Hunter made a mental note to seek out the lady at his first available opportunity. He had many aversions but attractive women had never been one of them. 'She kept her head and stayed right calm,' continued the driver. 'And this gent was real handy with that fancy pistol of his.' Again Hunter took note. A 'fancy pistol' could mean a fancy gunslinger.

'Me and Johnny was doing our best from underneath the coach, but it was only a matter of time. We couldn't have held out for too long. But we didn't have to as it happened.' The crowd of people gathered outside had been murmuring among themselves while the driver spoke but, at these words, they all became silent.

'What you mean?' asked a voice.

'Like I said,' came back the answer. 'We didn't have to do no waiting. Someone stopped 'em 'fore they had time to wear us down.'

'That's right,' said a musical and cultured feminine voice with just a faint trace of a Scandinavian accent. 'You pray hard for a miracle just as I was when crouching low in a corner of the coach. But when it happens you find it almost impossible to believe or accept it.'

'The lady's smack on,' interrupted the driver. 'It was a miracle.' He had an audience hanging onto his every word and he was making the most of it. Hunter smiled to himself. He had been called a lot of things in his life to date but never once had he been described as a miracle.

'A miracle?' demanded someone else from the crowd. 'What the hell you talking about?'

'You doubting the lady's word?' roared the driver.

'Not hers. Just yours!' replied a wag from the far side of the gathering. The people around him laughed loudly but without malice.

'I'll settle your hash afterwards Barney boy,' yelled the driver. 'Right now I'm gonna finish what I've got to say if it takes all afternoon.'

'And it probably will,' interjected the man he had called 'Barney boy'. 'All the hot air ain't in the desert right now that's for damn sure.'

Ignoring a further outburst of laughter the driver continued his story. 'It was just one man. No more. You could tell that by the spacing of his shots. All from the same area and all making the same sound. Four shots. That's all it took. Four shots and he killed all four of 'em. Johnny an' me took a look at 'em up in the rocks before we came back to town with what was left of the mule team. Each of 'em had a bullet in his chest. Right where it counted most.'

'Did you get a look at the man who shot them?' asked a voice. Hunter recognised it as that of Buckner.

'No sir Mr Buckner. He was at least a quarter-mile off. I never seen shooting like it in all my life. And that includes a five-year hitch in the army. There was some better-than-average shots there I can tell you. But not one of 'em could handle a rifle the way this man did. It was more than human. I just never seen anything like it afore.'

'Did you recognise any of the dead men you and Johnny saw up in the rocks?' asked Buckner.

'No, not one of 'em. Looked a pretty rough bunch to me. Couldn't bring 'em into town on the stage because of the passengers. So if you want a look at 'em I guess the sheriff had better bring 'em in right off afore the buzzards peck 'em beyond recognition.'

Hunter leaned out of his window casually. 'Did I hear someone mention me?' he enquired. Without looking directly at her, he noticed that the woman passenger, although dust-stained from her journey and recent ordeal, possessed a dignity rare among women in this part of the country. She was also very beautiful with blonde hair which was in accord with the slightly Scandinavian accent he had detected in her voice. Tall for a woman, almost his own height in fact, her beauty was coldly classical. Like a statue meticulously sculptured to order rather than one carved with the full warmth of a sculptor who has created for love alone.

'Yes sheriff you did,' answered Buckner. 'Four owlhoots tried to hold up the stage but got shot for their efforts. "Bull" Stander, he's the driver, thinks you ought to go an' bring 'em in. I think he's right an' I'll go along with you. It might just be that one of us might've seen one or more of them at some time or another somewhere.'

'I will be down immediatedly,' said Hunter. He noticed that the 'gent with the fancy pistol' was looking up at him with more than a casual interest. The curiosity with which one professional always views another of the same kind, he thought. The man, in his early forties, was a little more than six feet tall, slimly built, but not without a suggestion of hidden strength. His face had character. It appeared serious, yet there was humour written clearly in its eyes for anyone who bothered to read them. He was as well dressed as Hunter but the gun he carried in the traditional thigh holster was far more ostentatious than the one the marshal used.

It was difficult to see exactly what type of handgun the man carried as it was half-hidden by the holster but it appeared to be an up-to-date version of the Colt .44 with an ivory handle and silver or silver-plated metalwork. Most of the men Hunter had encountered who wore such flashy sideguns rarely knew how to use them well. Such weapons were merely symptomatic of their inflated egos.

Here was an exception, however. An egotist perhaps. But one who could make good whatever boasts he made concerning his capabilities with a gun. A man to be wary of. A showy gun in the hand of a man who knew how to shoot a pistol fast and accurately had always meant trouble in Hunter's experience.

It was possible he was wrong but, in this game, to gamble was often to lose. The stakes were always too high for Hunter to gamble unless there was no other way out. Life was too good to throw away like money in a game of chance. He lived dangerously. To him this was life. There was no other way of living it. But never recklessly. That was stupid.

These thoughts were moving almost unconsciously through his mind as he put on his tie and jacket, brushed his clothes, checked his revolver, replaced it in its holster, straightened his jacket to avoid the gun making a bulge, and walked downstairs.

Buckner was waiting for him at the bottom of the stairs. With him were the stage driver, the guard, both passengers and a scattering of interested onlookers. The remainder had seen and heard enough and gone back to work or to their homes.

'Allow me to introduce our sheriff.' Buckner turned first to the beautiful young woman with the Scandinavian accent. 'Miss er . . .'

'Johansson. Miss Helga Johansson.' She smiled as she spoke. For a woman who had been through so much she displayed remarkable courage and composure, thought Hunter.

'Miss Johansson,' continued Buckner. 'This is the sheriff of Broken Leg, Mr Hunter.'

'It is good to know you Mr Hunter.' She smiled again and extended her right hand. Hunter shook it. She had a firm and warm grip.

'It is also a pleasure to meet you Miss Johansson,' returned Hunter. 'Despite the dust of your journey and the strain of your terrible experience you are obviously a very beautiful woman. However, before we speak any further I think perhaps you would prefer to have a bath to freshen yourself. You look very tired.'

'You are most gallant sheriff. Yes. I do feel tired and I would like a bath.'

Buckner was angry at himself for not being the first to think of her personal comfort. However, the shadow that crossed his face was a brief one. He dispersed it by ordering the hotel clerk, Wooller, to arrange hot water for a bath for Miss Johansson. 'And have a clean room ready for her immediatedly,' he added.

'Yes sir.' The clerk walked away to do as he was told.

Buckner now turned to the other passenger from the coach. 'Perhaps you would also like a bath Mr . . .'

'Patterson. William Patterson. Yes I would like a bath. And a room also for I intend staying in Broken Leg for a while.'

'William Patterson,' mused Buckner. 'You wouldn't be the Bill Patterson by any chance?'

'The same.'

'You know him?' interrupted Miss Johansson.

'By reputation only Miss,' replied Buckner. 'From all I've heard of him he's the best with a gun in this and many other parts of the country with the possible exception of the sheriff here. And equally at home with a deck of cards. That right Mr Patterson?'

'So they tell me. But you have things in the wrong order. I am a professional gambler first. I enjoy handling cards much more than handling a gun. Any expertise I may have acquired with the gun is simply the result of defending myself against the troublemakers one always finds in a game of cards.'

'Always?' queried Miss Johansson.

'There are exceptions of course. But, unfortunately,

they are rare. In most games there is generally at least one person who should not be playing. Either because he does not like losing or because he cannot afford to lose. And, one thing I would like you to believe, despite anything you may have heard to the contrary, is that I never cheat at cards. I don't have to.

'Gambling is as good a way of making money as any I know. For as they say "fools and their money are soon parted". And most men who gamble are fools. Unlike a truly professional card player, they never weigh the odds scientifically. So, I never have any feelings of guilt when taking their money. If I didn't take it then someone else would. You will never stop men gambling. But one thing is certain; although I have defended myself successfully with this gun on a number of occasions, I would never use it for monetary reward.'

He looked across at Hunter and held out his hand. 'No offence intended sheriff.'

Hunter found himself looking at the other man in a new light. 'None taken,' he replied calmly, shaking the gambler's hand. 'But for a man who does not seek trouble you wear a very decorative weapon which would seem to invite it.'

'It's all part of the act sheriff. A revolver less ... er ... decorative, as you put it, would be just as effective in a nasty situation I admit. But people would feel disappointed. Let down. They expect a gambler to be dressed immaculately, with a fancy silk waistcoat, wear a diamond stick-pin in his tie and carry showy weapons. And, one thing I learned early in this business, never disappoint the customers. Never give them less than they expect. You'll never attract them or their money if you do. A gambler in a faded shirt and torn jeans would get few people to sit in on any game with him no matter how good he was with the cards.'

'But don't you ever get called out by any of these young gunnies out to make a quick reputation?' asked Buckner. 'You make an inviting target.'

'Several times. But never one occasion that I couldn't walk away from. I don't mind being called a coward. Name-calling has never spoiled my reputation. These gun-happy kids on the prowl are anxious to prove something. I don't have to.

'No, I've only shot men who were really trying to kill me anyway they knew how. These kids want a head-on showdown with an even-chance draw. They're not out to kill you no matter what. That wouldn't give them a reputation. It has to be on even terms. It's easy to walk away from a set-up like that. Pride is seldom worth getting killed for. Or a good enough reason for killing someone else. Most blood shed only for this reason is a waste and totally unnecessary.'

'Then why come to a wide-open town like Broken Leg which has got more than its fair share of these trigger-happy kids you're talking about?' queried Buckner.

'You have answered your own question,' replied Patterson. 'Simply because it is wide-open. Where else would there be such easy money for a man with my talents?'

'You got me there,' admitted Buckner. 'You got a point.'

# Chapter Six

Hunter and Buckner trotted their mounts casually along the road the stage had followed into town. Buckner was astride a superb looking white stallion. The horse was as much a part of Buckner's vanity as anything else he owned. It had been groomed until every hair gleamed in the sunlight. Its appearance was faultless and it was a good enough horse. Yet it lacked the strength and endurance of Hunter's wiry brown mustang.

Both men rode in silence for a while. A serenity ruled over everything in sight. All around seemed totally tranquil and pure. Not even a solitary wisp of cloud marred the flawless blue of the sky above them. The air was dry but crisp and clean. Hunter thrived in such surroundings. Even Buckner was impressed. Hence the silence.

As they rode into the canyon where the attack on the coach had taken place Buckner was the first to speak. 'That's where it happened.' He pointed to an area in the centre of the canyon. The two dead mules had been pulled to one side to allow free passage for anyone riding this same road but the marks on the ground told the story even more eloquently than the stage driver.

Dark patches in the dust showed where the lead mules had first been hit. A few yards further on larger bloodstains and the deep gouges made in the earth by the threshing hooves of the two animals indicated precisely where they had been brought down finally by bullets from the rifles above. Indentations made by the coach's wheels, scuff marks caused by men crawling beneath it, splinters of wood from the bodywork of the stage and a number of spent cartridges told the remainder of the story.

'Bull, Johnny an' that gambler Patterson must've put up a helluva scrap,' commented Buckner.

'It certainly looks that way,' agreed Hunter. 'If it had been an even fight instead of an ambush I think they might well have managed without any outside help.'

'Outside help,' mused Buckner, dismounting. 'I'd almost forgot that. Let's go up an' have a look at them boys up there.'

Hunter jumped lightly from his mustang and ground-tethered both animals. Buckner had already started to scramble up one side of the canyon so Hunter followed him. At the top the big man paused for breath. Hunter pretended to be slightly winded as well although the climb, in fact, had taken nothing from him. Never let an opponent know what cards you are holding, he thought. And his magnificient fitness was always his trump card in any really tight game. So he never played it until whoever he was up against was in too deep to extricate himself without losing.

'Let's spread out a bit and see if we can spot 'em,' said Buckner. 'Should't be too difficult. There's not too much space up here.'

Hunter knew where the bodies would be if they had not been moved, so he manoeuvred in such a way that the other man found them first.

'They're over here!' called Buckner. Hunter joined him

behind a cluster of boulders. 'Sure was pretty shootin'. Just like Bull said. What do you think Hunter?'

'To be honest it baffles me completely. I have no idea who could have killed them or why they held up the stage in the first instance. I understand that it never carries anything other than passengers and mail.'

'Hunter, I think by now I ought to be able to trust you a bit more than when you first started workin' for me. So here's how it is. You're right up to a point. Normally that stage does carry only passengers, mail an' the suchlike. But just once in a while it also carries an extra box for me. Bull and Johnny must have guessed what is in it by now but I pay 'em more than enough to keep quiet.' He hesitated briefly.

Hunter did not interrupt. He had a feeling, similar to the instinct of an animal, which told him to say nothing and just listen. It told him that here was coming the opening through which he could enter Buckner's business of gun-running.

The other continued: 'That box is used very little. When it is used it is only for carrying money, always in gold, from some business associates up north. This time it was bringing me ten thousand in twenty-dollar pieces. Now, what I can't figure out is how in the hell they knew it was on the stage. It don't figure at all. Bull an' Johnny was too close to getting' killed to be in on something like this.'

'Why gold?' asked Hunter. 'Why not a bank draft? It's a great deal safer.'

'Yeah, I know. But I got a big deal goin' an' the people I do business with won't play it that way.'

'Make them,' argued Hunter. 'It is perfectly legal.'

Buckner flared up. 'There's only one thing wrong with

your figuring boy. My business ain't perfectly legal. So they got the whip-hand. Understand?'

'I am beginning to. And it leads to two possibilities.'

'Which are?' interrupted Buckner impatiently.

Working on the principle of 'divide and conquer', Hunter answered: 'That either your business associates who send you the money, or those who receive it from you, arranged the hold-up. Or, a third possibility, both ends.'

'Now why in the hell should they do that?'

'Greed, Mr Buckner. One of the oldest and most powerful motives ever to guide the thinking of civilised men. If such was the case in this instance, then the objective of those involved would be simply to force out the middle-man, namely yourself.'

'By stealing their own gold? It don't make sense.'

'Not their gold,' corrected Hunter. 'Your gold. It is carried on your stage. When the money is at neither one end nor the other then it is entirely your responsibility is it not? How long could you continue to sustain such losses?'

Buckner was following Hunter's chain of thought with ease by now. 'By God you could be right, damn their hides. Both ends, as you call 'em, know the set-up as well as I do. So my business partners up north, who been puttin' up some of the money, could push me out easy enough and handle it all themselves. It would take some time to bust me money-wise but they could make it look like I was mishandling things. That way they could take my cut.

'An' if it was those I buy the goods from they could sell direct at the same price I do an' take my profits along with their own.'

Still employing the technique of 'divide and conquer',

Hunter quietly added: 'Plus the money that would have been taken from the stage and which you would have had to make good yourself if the attack had proved successful. As I have stated; either end or both ends. No matter who, only you stand to lose. No one else. You have admitted that all transactions are in cash. You could prove nothing against the other parties involved in this business. So neither end would care. They simply do not need you. Regrettable. But a fact.'

'Could be. But just one thing puzzles me. I'm the one with connections in Mexico. How in the hell they goin' to sell those guns without me?'

'Guns?'

'Yes, guns dammit. Now you know boy. I sell guns to the Mex's. Christ, if I didn't do it someone else would. You can't stop greasers killing each other. God almighty it's become a national pastime.'

'So we have yet another possibility in that case,' interjected Hunter. 'Another group with a ready market, probably also in Mexico, who would like to take over your source of supply. And as the first move has been made against you already we must assume, if this new possibility is a correct assumption, that they now have positive knowledge of your source.'

'You think good Hunter. You got a real head on your shoulders I could do with all your savvy right now. You fancy being cut in on the deal in return for that savvy of yours?'

'Right now, however, it is not a very promising deal is it? So I would have to know a little more about the operation before giving a reply.'

'Fire the questions. I'll shoot back what answers I can,' said Buckner.

'Well, firstly, who are your business associates in the north who contribute towards the cost of buying the guns?'

'You ain't gonna believe this boy but it's the North-East Industrial and Commercial Finance Corporation. Big eh?'

'The biggest I believe,' replied Hunter calmly and made a mental note for his superiors in Washington. 'And the name of the firm which sells you the guns?'

'No firm. I get 'em from the commanding officer of Fort Bantock. Him and his adjutant slide 'em out a few at a time and then write 'em off in the books as unserviceable or lost.' Hunter made another mental note. 'Neat, ain't it?' added Buckner. 'Until now that is. That's why I need your brains. I know my limits. I'm clever enough in most ways but I ain't in their class. You are. So how about it? You want it or not? An' if you don't want in an' ever go against me I'll deny sayin' anything to you. It'd be just your word against mine. Well?'

'What would be my share?' enquired Hunter casually.

'Ten per cent. That's about five thousand dollars a year.'

'Not enough,' stated Hunter just as calmly. 'Make it double that figure. Twenty per cent and I will accept.'

'Christ Hunter, you stomp a man hard when he's down. But we both know I need you so I agree.' He held out his hand and Hunter shook it.

'How do you know you can trust me?' asked Hunter.

'I don't know. But I do know you're not stupid. I got no idea who's crossing me up right now, but if you did the same I'd know it soon enough an' have you shot by the boys like you was some crazy dog.'

'You have a point there,' conceded Hunter. 'It would be rather stupid of me would it not?'

'You can bet your life on that. Come to think of it that's exactly what you would be doin' ain't it,' said Buckner and laughed. He became serious again. 'Now, what you got in mind we should do about this trouble?'

'Simple answer: eliminate the trouble-makers. I take it that you do not know either of these men.' He looked down at the two corpses.

Buckner shook his head. 'Never even seen 'em before.'

'Then let us look at the two on the other side. There is a chance that you may recognise one or both of them.' They climbed back down in silence.

As they strode across the canyon floor again prior to ascending the far side, Hunter commented: 'Incidentally, I trust you realise that a sheriff's jurisdiction does not extend beyond the limits of the town which makes him a law officer. I have no official status out here.'

'Hell, I know that. But this was personal. I knew what was on that stage and I wanted you out here with me. You and that thinkin' brain of yours.' He grinned. 'Got any ideas?'

'Only one.'

'An' what's that?' grunted Buckner.

'Simply the course of action we should follow.'

'Don't talk in riddles. I got little enough breath left with all this damn climbing without havin' to keep asking you questions. Talking plain for God's sake – and for mine.'

'Well, if you do not know either of the two men on the opposite side I think you should send someone out with a wagon to take them into town. It is possible that somebody there may have seen one or more of them before.'

'And if no one does know 'em?'

'Then I suggest you get really tough. Word will soon spread about the attack on the stage. Make sure it reaches your partners at either end of the operation. Then employ large escorts to accompany the stage on its run each week whether it is carrying money for you or not.

'This will accomplish at least three things. It will make you appear public-spirited as only a few of us know what the protection is really for. It will avoid the suspicion you would arouse if you used the escort for selected runs only. And it will let the people responsible for the attack know that you really mean business.'

'An' what if it don't?'

'It will. The size and type of escort I have in mind would frighten away even a fair-sized army patrol.'

Buckner grinned. 'Now you're talkin' language I can understand. One thing though. Where's the extra money comin' from for this armed escort you got in mind?'

'As I said, make sure that word of this attack reaches your partners – all of them. I feel certain they would wish to come to a quick financial agreement rather than lose a share in the lucrative business you are running for them. Take the initiative. Put the pressure on them for a change. If one really thinks about the situation seriously enough you are in a better bargaining position than any of them.'

'I am? How?'

'For the simple reason that they all stand to lose a great deal more than you. Positions of authority and power in either civil or military life. Situations in which they can make, in fact already are making, vast sums of money. As far as you are concerned, one part of the world is much the same as the next. If you were forced to move it would affect you very little.'

By this time both men had crossed the floor of the canyon. There were no further words from either of them until they had scrambled up the far wall and were looking at the bodies of the other two ambushers. Buckner shook his head. 'No,' he said breathlessly following the exertion of the climb. 'Never seen either one before.'

'Well, you will have to send out a wagon for them and see if anyone in town recognises any of the four. However, we may never know who sent them. Not that it matters really. The new policy will stop any possible recurrence of this nature.'

'Come again son?'

Hunter smiled. 'It will not happen again now that the coach will be protected on every run by a force of armed guards with an experienced scout always in the lead.'

Buckner shrugged. 'Still puzzles me though who in the hell stopped 'em? And why? What do you reckon? Bronco Apache out to kill a few white men all legal for a change? There are still a few Apache bucks around who ain't been tamed.'

Hunter smiled again. 'That just might be the answer. But I have a feeling you will never know for certain. Just be thankful. We both owe him, whoever he was, a great deal.'

'Both of us? queried Buckner.

'Naturally,' replied Hunter. 'He saved your ten thousand dollars. And that means he also saved me twenty per cent of whatever you turn your share of that money into.'

'My God boy. You ever wrong? You got an answer for everything. Come on we got to climb down this damn mountain again and I'm willin' to bet you ain't got an easy answer for that.'

'I am afraid I will have to refuse that wager,' replied Hunter with a grin. 'However, there is a much quicker way down.'

'There is?' queried Buckner. 'What?'

'Jump. But as it is not an easier way I would have lost the bet.'

Now Buckner smiled. 'Some risk you'd be taking. If I jumped how in thunder would I collect my winnings?'

'You have a very valid point,' conceded Hunter as they commenced the downward climb.

# Chapter Seven

No one in Broken Leg recognised any of the bodies so Hunter's plan was put in operation. 'Bull' still drove the coach on its weekly run and Johnny still went with him as shotgun guard. This was just a gesture, however, because a small army of men, hand-picked by Hunter, gave the stage all the protection it was ever likely to need. Two men flanked either side of the coach while six more rode in front and six others to the rear. Two or three hundred yards ahead rode the scout, always in sight of the men behind him.

All seventeen men, this included the scout, were mounted on the best horses available in the area and each man was armed according to Hunter's instructions. This meant that every rider in the escort not only carried a side arm but also an 1894 model Winchester .30–30 with an eight-shot tubular magazine.

Before hiring any of them Hunter had insisted that each passed a rigorous series of test with both horse and weapons. He had demanded this for two reasons. Superficially, he wanted Buckner to see how thorough he was. If he was ever going to break this man he hated so much, and stop him trading guns into Mexico, then he was going to have to gain his confidence completely. There would be no other way of catching Buckner off-guard. Hunter knew this.

His second reason was far more devious and entirely personal. He wanted to see how every man performed with his guns so that if he ever had to go against any of them he would know exactly how proficient each man was. That would give him, Hunter, an even greater edge than he already had over any of them individually. Or more than one, if the need arose, he thought grimly.

After the tenth consecutive run by the stage without any further trouble, both Buckner and Hunter began to breathe a little easier. And, just as Hunter had predicted, all Buckner's partners were more than eager to contribute towards the cost of the armed escort, either to protect their interests or to avert suspicion from themselves. No matter what the reason, however, Hunter's plan had proved successful.

Hunter grinned as his twenty per cent began to accumulate into a worthwhile sum in a bank which he knew to be absolutely safe. His superior had told him, unofficially of course, that he could pursue any method he had to in order to bring the gun-running to a standstill. Well, he was doing simply that. So whatever money was in his account at the end of this business would be his – officially! There would be nothing the department could do about it without losing its best operative and a huge portion of its reputation. No, the department would never let itself be caught with its fingers in the till.

What had the chief said before Hunter left Washington? 'Be your usual smooth, underhanded, conniving self and I'll be more than happy.' Well, he had no intention of disappointing the old man.

Neither did he intend disappointing his superior where the gun-running was concerned. Hunter was confident that he could stop it. But to do so entailed the necessity of joining one of Buckner's expeditions into Mexico. Without this he would be unable to uncover the complete operation and any success achieved, therefore, would be only partial. It had to be total. Anything less would be failure. To go on at least one expedition was absolutely essential.

Since the attack on the stagecoach there had been two such trips across the border. He had hinted on both occasions, albeit not too forcefully as he wished to avoid any possible suspicion being directed his way, that it would be beneficial to business if he went along once in a while.

However, Buckner had refused to bite. Hunter could not fault the other man's thinking. To let any one person know his entire operation would be to hand it to that same person on a plate. As Buckner had no intention of doing this he always kept the Mexican side of things to himself alone. Even the men who delivered the guns for him knew nothing other than where the arms were handed over. And even this was changed from time to time so that the exact destination always remained unknown to them until the last possible moment.

All Hunter could do was wait for the right opportunity to arise. So he waited. There was no alternative. Buckner was far too cagey.

The break for which Hunter had been waiting came abruptly and dramatically.

He was seated comfortably in the hotel dining room enjoying a late evening meal when one of Buckner's hardcases strode in. 'You're wanted at the ranch,' he told Hunter.

Hunter looked up casually. 'Where are your manners

man? Were you never taught that it is extremely rude to interrupt a person who is eating?'

The man's bravado disappeared immediately. He had seen Hunter in action on a couple of occasions. 'Sorry sheriff. No offence. But Mr Buckner would like to see you out at the ranch.' He was referring to the collection of wooden structures where the wagons used for gun-running were housed.

'When?'

'He says to come right now Mr Hunter. He said to tell you it was urgent.'

Hunter placed his knife and fork carefully together on his still half-full plate and wiped his mouth with the table napkin provided. Slowly easing back his chair, he stood up. 'Then I suppose I shall have to ride with you and find out what Mr Buckner wants,' he remarked with apparent disinterest. But well-hidden beneath his cool exterior was a warm glow of anticipation. He was a creature of instinct as well as logic.

As the ranch was barely a half-mile south of the town, it took but a few minutes of riding to reach there.

'They're in there.' Hunter's riding companion indicated the huge barn which accommodated the wagons. The marshal had already noticed that this was the only building with a light showing.

Whatever Hunter had prepared himself for it certainly was not the gruesome sight which waited him as he entered the barn. The woman from the coach, Helga Johansson, sprawled grotesquely on the floor like a life-size rag doll. She had been beaten to death. Her clothes, almost in shreds, were covered with blood.

He had seen worse during his career which, of necessity, had been intertwined inextricably on many occasions with moments of terrible violence. But, somehow, this once beautiful, now hideous, sight stretched out on the ground at his feet affected him deeply. His face betrayed nothing. It was empty of any emotion whatsoever as he looked up at the dozen or so men standing around the body.

Buckner spoke. 'We found them here after one of the boys I left on watch reported seeing two people searchin' the ranch.'

'Two?' queried Hunter.

Buckner pointed to a dimly lit corner of the building. 'Him as well,' he said.

Hunter peered into the semi-darkness. The gambler, Patterson, was seated on the floor with his back propped up against a sack of grain. He was in a similar condition to the girl with the exception that he was breathing still. But he was unconscious and not far from death. The marshal knew how close to it Patterson was for he had experienced like scenes many, far too many, times before.

He turned to face Buckner. 'But why this? What had they done to make you do this to them?'

Buckner answered in a manner that made it appear as if what had taken place was an everyday occurrence. 'Well, to be honest, they wouldn't tell us at first. In fact it took a hell of a lot of persuasion as you can see. I'm sorry about the girl. She was a real looker. But we would have had to kill 'em afterwards anyway you look at it.'

'But why?' Hunter's voice was as steady as a rock and just as hard.

If Buckner noticed the hardness he thought it was directed at the two on the floor. 'They were spies,' he replied casually. 'Spying for Diaz and his cronies in Mexico City. They had found out too much. We couldn't let 'em live. Look around you Hunter. This place is packed with guns, ammunition and powder. We were going to make a trip across the border in a week or so.'

'Were?' queried Hunter.

Buckner's reply was interrupted by a groan from Patterson who had returned to consciousness. Hunter walked across and squatted on his haunches in front of the dying man. The gambler looked up at him and spoke with difficulty through swollen and cut lips which he somehow managed to twist into a cynical smile. '. . . never hired my guns out before. First time . . . and . . .' His words turned into a terrible groan of intense pain. 'Oh my God . . . and this happens.' He spoke no more before dying a few seconds later.

Hunter turned towards Buckner. 'Whatever he may have been he was certainly no spy. What did he mean about hiring out his guns for the first time?'

'Quite true apparently. Stuck to his story anyway. Despite what the boys did to help loosen his tongue. The woman was the spy. She hired him for protection. After all, it is a rough part of the country sheriff.'

'Rough it may be. But few men take kindly to other men who beat a woman to death,' Hunter pointed out. 'Particularly a beautiful woman. Not even in this part of the country. So how are you going to explain this away?'

'I won't have to. If you remember I told you that we had intended to take another shipment of stuff south in about a week.'

'That is correct. You did. But you said "were" and not "are" did you not?'

'A good memory. Yes I did,' replied Buckner. 'We're bringing the trip forward. Tonight in fact.'

'Tonight? But why?' asked Hunter, sensing that this

201

man he had hated for so long was now about to slip away unscathed only to recommence his criminal activities elsewhere.

'Because it just ain't healthy here no more. Diaz must know something or she . . .' he indicated the dead woman with the toe of his boot, '. . . wouldn't have got this close. No Hunter, we move now. What with this, and the stage hold-up, only a fool would stay. A man's gotta know when to move on. So tonight we take everything we got and head into Mexico.'

'And then?'

Buckner lowered his voice so only Hunter could hear him. 'Who knows? I've known this would have to happen sometime so I've been selling off my property in town on the quiet. A little at a time. The money's safely tucked away in a bank someplace else. And when I've sold this lot tonight I'll be sitting a damn sight more than pretty.'

Hunter's mind was working rapidly. How could he stop this man before he reached his Mexican contacts? He knew he might not get a second chance. Like most other people he believed in luck. He had enjoyed his share of it. But he was not fool enough ever to rely upon its intervention. Then, a faint glimmer of hope. 'Incidentally, why did you call me out here tonight?' he asked casually. 'You could have ridden away and taken my share of the money on this deal with you. Why did you not do so?'

Buckner studied him carefully for a few seconds before answering. 'Two reasons. One, I don't think anyone rides away from you. Not for long anyway. Two,' he lowered his voice still further. 'I don't trust any of this bunch not to jump me once I've got the cash for this delivery.

They'd think a sight different, I reckon, if you were riding with me. They know your reputation. They all seen you fight. Ain't one of 'em not afraid of you. And I figure you'll want to come along and protect your interests . . .'

The men had already started to load the wagons at a signal from Buckner. Hunter was noting, without appearing to, what was being piled into the three vehicles. He saw with satisfaction that the ammunition and kegs of powder had been distributed fairly evenly among the wagons. This made all three vulnerable to a plan of attack now formulating in his mind.

'So can I count on you Hunter?' asked Buckner.

'You can,' was the even reply. 'When I set out to accomplish anything I invariably succeed.'

'Good.'

Buckner strolled across to the wagons to ensure that they were being loaded securely. Hunter followed him to see what types of weapons were being sold currently in Mexico. The consignment was mainly of rifles. In fact he could see no side-arms whatever. The majority of the rifles were Springfield .45–70 single-shot carbines. This had been the standard weapon of the United States army for years.

It was an unsettling thought that such guns could be obtained so easily for sale in Mexico. But what was even more disturbing was the presence of several crates of Krags. The Krag, or Krag-Jorgensen after its Norwegian inventors, was the U.S. Magazine Rifle model 1892 and was the army's latest repeater. It fired either a .30–40 Krag cartridge or the U.S. Army clibre .30, the first smokeless service cartridge ever used by the United States armed forces.

His thoughts were interrupted by Buckner's booming

voice. 'Swires, Wilson, Bell. You three get some shovels, take these bodies outside in the corral and bury 'em. Make it deep and let the horses stomp the ground afterwards. I don't want any wild animals diggin' 'em up after we've gone an' I don't want any traces left for no busybodies to follow-up.'

# Chapter Eight

The wagons trundled along quietly through the night. The wheels of all three vehicles were muffled, as were the hooves of the mules and horses. The moon was not yet full. Buckner had told Hunter earlier that he preferred to ride when the moon gave most light. 'But we got no choice this time,' he had added.

Now, as they rode alongside one another, Buckner explained: 'Night is always the best time to move anything illegal across the border; anyone knows that. The guards are either asleep or afraid. But most people prefer it dark. Not me. The lighter the night, the easier it is to move quietly.' He chuckled. 'You can't see a damn thing when it's dark. Keep banging into things. Never saw sense in that. Also, less chance of an ambush when you can see what's ahead. And a better chance of running for it if there is one.'

Hunter noticed that Buckner played it carefully in case of attack. He always rode well to the rear. If anyone jumped the column he was in a position to be first away from the line of fire. 'But not this time,' Hunter added grimly to himself.

He had no foreknowledge of the route they were following but the rate at which they were moving indicated that those in front had travelled it more than once before. All he could do was wait.

Knowing exactly where the powder kegs were situated in each of the wagons, he was waiting for them to veer either right or left somewhere along the trail so that all three would be broadside-on across his front. A few well-placed shots from his rifle would then complete his mission. With the moon three-quarters full, and the added advantage of his cat-like vision at night, it would be easier than knocking down metal ducks in a fairground shooting gallery. And the men were bunched far too close to the wagons for any of them to escape the consequent explosions.

After seeing the result of what they had done to Helga Johansson, Hunter felt no qualms whatever. From a practical angle, it also meant that when he rode away afterwards he would not have to keep looking back to see if any of them were trailing him. It would be a 'fait accomplis'. With the exception of Buckner, however. For he continued to ride well to the rear of the wagons, although his horse had now moved slightly ahead of the marshal's mount.

Hunter anticipated and savoured the pleasure of dealing with this man separately.

Almost an hour passed before the wagons started moving into the type of position for which Hunter had been waiting. After turning fractionally left to avoid a large outcrop of rock, the three vehicles started veering to their right again. As the angle became more acute he made his move.

Buckner was now several yards ahead and did not see Hunter move into the shadows of the rocks and slide his .303 Savage from its saddle holster. The wagons were little more than a hundred yards away and all were strung neatly across his field of fire.

Six shots shattered the stillness of the night in less than the same number of seconds. The wagons exploded instantaneously like three enormous bombs. Balls of fire leaped skywards, as though discharged from gigantic Roman candles. The area was lit up as if dawn had arrived hours earlier than it should have done.

Men, horses and mules alike screamed in absolute terror. As terrifying as they were, these cries were soon over. The only sounds left were those made by rounds of ammunition exploding from the crates on the wagons, the hungry roar of the flames as they swiftly devoured the wooden vehicles and their contents and the panic-stricken voice of Buckner as he urged his mount into full flight.

Hunter reholstered his rifle and drew his Parker 10-gauge sawn-off shotgun from the other side of his saddle. Within seconds he was spurring his horse after Buckner.

At this point he could not see him. But he could hear him and that was sufficient. Even if the horses had been an equal match in speed and endurance, the marshal would have had the edge in any race against the man ahead. Buckner was riding wildly. Hunter rode with cold deliberation.

The chase ended in a small arroyo which came to a sudden end. Buckner whirled his horse, snatched his rifle from its scabbard alongside the saddle and jumped to the ground. He squeezed his bulky frame behind a group of boulders and waited.

Knowing that Buckner was not aware of who had fired the shots which had blown up the wagons, Hunter rode calmly into the arroyo. 'Is that you Mr Buckner?' he called. 'It's me. Hunter.'

Buckner came from behind the rocks with a sigh of

relief. 'Thank God. I heard someone following me. At least I thought I did. But I didn't know who.' He was breathing heavily from the exertion of the ride and was covered in a greyish dust. 'What the hell happened back there? Jesus Christ, what a mess! Must have been a small army of 'em.'

Hunter said nothing. With the shotgun tucked casually under his left arm he dismounted. With his free hand he took a canteen of water from his saddle horn. 'You look as if you need this,' he said quietly, offering the canteen to Buckner.

The other man relaxed a little, placed his rifle against a rock and reached out for the water. Hunter dropped the canteen to the ground and transferred the Parker 10-gauge to his right hand in one swift movement. Buckner was so bewildered that he made no attempt to pick up his rifle. Hunter kicked it away.

'Now take your revolver gently from its holster and drop it.' Buckner hesitated for a few seconds but, realising the futility of going against the shotgun, did as he was told. Hunter kicked the handgun away just as he had the rifle.

'Are you mad Hunter?' demanded Buckner, a mixture of anger and uncertainty in his voice.

In reply Hunter took from an inside pocket of his jacket a silver-plated badge engraved with the words 'U.S. Marshal'. 'Buckner, I am arresting you on a charge of gun-running,' he said quietly.

Buckner saw the shield in the pale light of the moon and was suddenly afraid but tried to act otherwise. He had seen Hunter in action. For once in Buckner's life physical violence was not the answer to the problem confronting him. 'You'll never make the charge hold in a court.' He attempted a laugh but failed dismally. 'You don't have any proof.'

'It is not going to court,' answered the lawman softly as he thumbed back the shotgun's two hammers. 'Because you are right. I cannot prove it. But I know you are guilty. And you know you are guilty. What else matters?'

'My God, you can't do it like this. You're a United States marshal. You've sworn to uphold the law, not break it.' His body started to tremble. Perspiration glistened on his forehead like so many pear-shaped glass beads. 'You are goin' to kill me aren't you. I can see it in your eyes. Oh Christ.' His voice was now as unsteady as his shaking body.

'Yes, I am going to kill you,' Hunter replied. The twin barrels of his shotgun still pointed unwaveringly at the other man's stomach.

Buckner's words attained a higher pitch as he approached hysteria. 'But why man? Good God, why?' Tears of sheer terror now began to mingle with the droplets of sweat running down his blood-drained face. 'You're a cultured man. Not a savage.'

His face took on a puzzled expression. 'This is something more than gun-running. This is personal isn't it? But why? Who in the hell are you? I never saw you before you started working for me.'

'You had seen me before. I could never forget your face. But you would not remember me. And as for who I am, you know that also. I am called Hunter.'

The gun-runner looked around in desperation. He was on the borderline of insanity. But not across it. He knew there would be no escape from those muzzles pointed at him. They would cut him to shreds.

He was now crying openly. 'I know your bloody name,' he sobbed, his voice cracking. 'But why, for the love of God, do you want to kill me?'

The other carried on as if he had not heard. 'Do you know that an Indian would not call me Hunter but He-Who-Hunts.'

'For Christ's sake man stop playing with me.'

Again the lawman continued as if totally unaware of the interruption. 'The Chiricahua Apache term for He-Who-Hunts is Null-Zhey-He. But that would mean nothing to you would it? However, it is a fact that most Apaches prefer their names in Spanish. Something they learned from the Mexicans. Do you know the Spanish equivalent of my name?'

Buckner shook his head. He attempted to speak but the words were an incoherent babble of sound.

Hunter answered his own question. 'It is Cazador,' he said simply.

Absolute fear now shone in the other's eyes as he recognised the name. Yet still the words would not come.

'Yes, I named myself after my father Cazador. You remember him do you not? You called him a big crippled buck. The Mexican authorities paid you well for his scalp. Also for those of my mother and two sisters. And for many others taken on that raid which you led against my people.'

Buckner at length recovered his voice. The words poured forth like water through a broken dam. 'But that was a long time ago. I've got influence now where it counts. You couldn't get away with it. The law would catch you and hang you. They wouldn't let an Indian . . .'

Hunter cut him short. 'I think not. For am I not a cultured man as you stated a short time ago? Only you know I am an Apache and a man's private knowledge also dies when he dies, does it not?'

Buckner was held by a horrible fascination as Hunter continued. 'Fortunately not all white men are as you. For it was an American rancher who found me after I fled the massacre. He did not see a young savage when he caught me stealing food from his house just north of the border a week or so later. He saw only a hungry, frightened ten-year-old boy. He fed and clothed me.

'For two years he and his Mexican wife cared for me and gave me a basic education. They even gave me their name although I no longer use it. They were good people but were past middle-age and knew that the harsh life they were leading had left them but a few years to live.

'So, when I was twelve, they sent me to an American school as their own son, using all the money they had saved to do so. I graduated with honours. I did it for them. Not for myself. It gave them something to be really proud of before they died. It gave them a sense of purpose and achievement that your kind could never even begin to understand Buckner. For it is those of your kind who are truly the savages of this world. It has nothing to do with the colour of a person's skin.

'That old man and his wife, each a different race and colour to the other, showed me that. I loved them both. And now I am more than grateful for what they did. Because I survive admirably in a world where others of my race are treated worse than animals.'

Hunter paused for a few seconds before continuing. 'I wanted you to know all these things before you died Buckner. You see I learned not only the white man's academic subjects. I learned also how to think as he does. All too often such thinking is entangled with deceit and

211

lies. And, because I absorbed these things so well, you will die and no one will ever know why it was or who did it.'

And he gently squeezed both triggers.